"I won't need you," she said sweetly, crossing her arms over her chest. "If I think about the history of our relationship, it's you that needs me."

Her arch question was met by complete silence. Morgan's dark blue eyes met hers, held, and she saw a flicker there, in the dark blue depths—a hot blue fire she'd never seen b

Jane Porter grew up on a diet of Harlequin Presents® romance novels, reading late at night under the covers so her mother wouldn't see! She wrote her first book at age eight and spent many of her high school and college years living abroad, immersing herself in other cultures and continuing to read voraciously. Now, Jane has settled down in rugged Seattle, Washington, with her gorgeous husband and two sons.

Jane loves to hear from her readers. You can write to her at P.O. Box 524, Bellevue, WA 98009, U.S.A. Or visit her Web site at www.janeporter.com.

Jane Porter

THE SECRETARY'S SEDUCTION

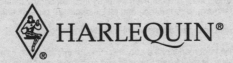

HARLEQUIN®

TORONTO • NEW YORK • LONDON
AMSTERDAM • PARIS • SYDNEY • HAMBURG
STOCKHOLM • ATHENS • TOKYO • MILAN • MADRID
PRAGUE • WARSAW • BUDAPEST • AUCKLAND

For my great friend, Barb. It is a fairy tale, isn't it?

ISBN 0-373-18847-1

THE SECRETARY'S SEDUCTION

First North American Publication 2005.

Copyright © 2002 by Jane Porter.

www.eHarlequin.com

Printed in U.S.A.

CHAPTER ONE

IT WAS sweltering. No one, but no one, married in Manhattan in the middle of July. No one but Winnie Graham that is.

The organist paused and the packed congregation in St. Paul's Cathedral seemed to rise in unison and all four hundred and fifty heads turned to stare at Winnie where she stood at the back of the church in her twenty-thousand-dollar silk bridal gown.

White silk gown.

Just like her white garter, white silk hose, white flowers, white carpet, white, white, white for a virgin bride.

For a twenty-five-year-old virgin bride who knew so little about life and men, that she was about to walk down the aisle without ever being kissed.

Well, she had been kissed once, *badly* kissed, back in seventh grade when Rufus Jones practically stuck his tongue down her throat at a junior high birthday party. She'd been so disgusted by the kiss that she'd nearly thrown up afterward, so that kiss didn't count.

And now she was about to marry the love of her life except he didn't love her and he'd never kissed her and she'd actually signed a contract agreeing to this horrible public society wedding which meant nothing to him.

What in God's name was she thinking? What in God's name was she doing?

How could she be a wife before she'd ever had a date?

Winnie closed her eyes, drew a deep breath and tried to calm herself but she was losing it, knew she was losing it. She was shaking so hard now she could barely keep her teeth from chattering. Funny how your teeth could chatter when you're burning up. Perspiration covered her skin. Her heart raced. She couldn't get enough air.

What a fool she was. What a perfect idiot.

Yes, she loved Morgan Grady. Yes, she was madly in love with Morgan Grady, but how could she sell herself like this? How could she sign away her life?

A contract.

She'd signed a contract to become his wife.

How could she love herself so little and him so much?

The organist struck the keys with fervor. Bars of music filled the cathedral, four hundred and fifty people seemed to inhale all at once, waiting for her to take the first step forward.

Winnie's head swam. The people became a blur of white noise and heat. It was so hot in here. There were too many people and not enough air. She felt as though she were suffocating. She couldn't breathe. Couldn't think. And they were all waiting for her to move. To take that first step. Morgan was waiting for her to take that first step.

So she did. She took a step, she turned around, she ran.

Winnie dropped her bouquet of white lilies, roses and orchids in the cool foyer, dashed through the cathedral's paneled doors, down the wide marble steps and jumped into a passing taxicab.

CHAPTER TWO

"WHERE to?" the cabdriver asked, sweating profusely and craning his head to get a look at her in the back seat, the stiff petticoats in her wedding gown making the white silk billow like huge sails on an eighteenth-century schooner.

The cabbie needed a shower. The inside of the car stank of old sweat. Winnie cranked her window down, dangerously close to throwing up.

"Anywhere," she choked, needing air, but the hot muggy air outside only made her more nauseous.

The driver shot her another glance. "I got to go somewhere, lady."

Where to go, where to go after leaving her family, Morgan and four hundred and fifty people behind in the church?

She had to go someplace that no one would find her. Someplace where no one would be. "The Tower, on Wall Street," she said, sinking against the seat, naming her office building.

It was Saturday, the office would be deserted, and not even Morgan would think to look for her there.

Closing her eyes, Winnie sagged against the sticky vinyl seat and tried to forget that she'd just run away from her own wedding, that she, Winnie Graham had left Morgan Grady, New York's Sexiest Bachelor, standing at the altar.

But eyes closed, she saw it all, saw how it happened.

She even knew the day—the hour—the moment—that everything in her life had changed.

June sixteenth. His office. Her insecurity.

"Willa, I need copies of these immediately," Morgan Grady said, thrusting a sheath of papers across the desk without looking up, "and the top two sets faxed to the client noted on the cover page."

Winnie's heart fell. Five and a half months she'd been working for him. Five and a half months and he still didn't know her name.

"It's Winnie," she corrected faintly, growing warm as color crept into her cheeks.

"What's that?"

She balled one hand and pressed her thumb across her knuckles. She'd never liked her name, never understood how her parents could look into her face as a newborn and think, *Winnie, yes, you with the little puffy eyes and tiny mouth, you're our Winnie.* But if Winnie was bad, Willa was far worse.

She'd corrected him before, several times actually, but he'd always been on his way in or out, or in the middle of something important, so she forgave the slips, and made up excuses for him.

But after five and a half months, the excuses had worn thin. Her patience had worn down. And her outer skin had worn *off.* She couldn't do this anymore, nor could she handle being invisible. It was definitely time to move on.

Winnie's lungs ached and she exhaled, feeling the elastic of her panty hose pinch her waist. She'd gained some weight over the winter, her usual extra five or ten pounds and she'd been slow to lose the weight this year. "You called me Willa."

He didn't look up. His attention never wavered from his Palm Pilot where he was making copious notes. "Yes."

Her panty hose was killing her. She couldn't remember when she felt so frumpy or dull. And worst of all, it wounded her pride that Mr. Grady was completely oblivious to her existence, while she knew—and was expected to know—*everything* about him.

Morgan Louis Grady. Born August first, Boston, Massachusetts.

A Leo, he took four newspapers daily, but didn't start reading until he'd hit his treadmill and weights for his morning workout.

He read all the important business sections of the paper between six and seven in the morning, during which he drank exactly two and a half cups of very strong, very black coffee. He had nothing until lunch— light salad and chicken from a caterer that delivered every day—and worked without interruption until three when she brought him a shot of espresso from the coffee cart downstairs.

Shirt size: sixteen and a half. Shoe size: eleven.

Height: six foot three. Weight: two hundred and five muscular pounds—*he* never varied in weight.

Impeccable dresser.

His hair was another matter. That couldn't, wouldn't be tamed. Thick, glossy and nearly black, he had a cowlick at his temple and he wore the back longer than the rest. He could cut it all short but he never did.

She knew all this, and more, and yet he didn't even know her name. Drawing a deep breath she blurted, "Mr. Grady, my name is Winnie, not Willa. I'm Winnie Graham and I've worked here since January second."

His dark head lifted. "Oh."

She stood a bit straighter, pulled back her shoulder blades, trying to project that she was taller, more impressive than her five feet, five inch height. "I replaced Miss Dirkle. And Miss Dirkle replaced Miss Hunts. And Miss Hunts, I believe, took over for Mrs. Amadio."

"Yes. Miss Dirkle, Miss Hunts, I remember."

They were making progress. Eye contact had been established. He recognized some names. He appeared to be listening. Good.

Now was the time to mention Friday.

Friday, four days from now, she had a final interview with a company in Charleston for a position much like the one she held now, executive assistant to the CEO of a major Fortune 500 firm. The job responsibilities and salary were equitable with what she had now, except that the cost of living in Charleston was much more affordable than Manhattan, and she'd be working for a kind, grandfather-like gentleman in his sixties rather than Morgan Grady, Wall Street's Most Eligible Bachelor. "About Friday, Mr. Grady—"

"What about Friday?"

"I sent you a memo."

"I don't recall."

There were moments she wondered how he could possibly be New York's youngest, shrewdest, most aggressive money manager. Everyone said he was brilliant. His firm received more press than any other investment firm on Wall Street, citing his leadership, insight and intuition, but he didn't display a bit of that insight and intuition with his assistant.

Flushing, Winnie pressed the stack of paperwork to her chest. "I left you a memo two weeks ago about needing Friday off, and then a follow up e-mail last week—"

"Sorry." He shook his head once, a short cryptic shake even as his gaze dropped to his desk and he reached for his phone. "Anyway, Friday's bad. Can't do. Wait until later in the summer, right?"

Wrong. Wrong, wrong, wrong. Not only had he said no, but she'd lost his attention.

Twenty seconds of conversation and he'd mentally checked out.

She glared at him, fighting tears, wondering just what went on inside that head.

He was heart-stoppingly beautiful. Women fell at his feet in droves.

Last year he'd even been voted Wall Street's Most Eligible Bachelor, six months ago he'd been selected New York's Sexiest Bachelor, and the florist deliveries continued to stream in. Long-stemmed red roses, potted palms, elegant orchids. Socialites, models, actresses, *other* men's wives…they all wanted him.

Including her.

She tried to study him dispassionately but there was nothing dispassionate about her feelings for him.

He had a great nose, a strong nose, with the smallest hump at the bridge and serious dark blue eyes, matched by the best mouth and most perfect chin in all of New

York. Correction, the most perfect face in all of New York.

Manhattan was the place of beautiful people and he was the most beautiful of all. But she couldn't handle it anymore, couldn't handle being a nothing, a nobody and so soon she'd be gone, off to another job, a slower pace of life, and an elderly white-haired, bespectacled boss.

"I can print off another memo, Mr. Grady. The original's still saved on my hard drive."

He shook his head, hung up the phone and began to place another call all without a glance in her direction. "Doesn't matter. Friday's not good."

"But I asked you two weeks ago." She heard her voice falter, and immediately strengthened it. "You didn't say no then."

"I didn't say anything at all."

"Exactly!"

"You can't take a non-answer as a yes."

"But, Mr. Grady—"

His dark head lifted abruptly. "Is this a family emergency?"

"No."

"Death in the family?"

"No."

"Death of a friend or former colleague?"

"No deaths. Personal leave."

He was staring at her and he had beautiful eyes, not exactly sapphire, more indigo, and when he looked at her like that, she could swear he saw straight through her. Literally. Straight through her to the wall behind her with the big clock and the fancy framed Chagall.

She'd lost him. He wasn't even thinking about her request. He was thinking numbers, odds, research, stocks, options, you name it, anything and everything but what she needed.

"Personal leave," he repeated softly, a crease between his brows.

"Yes, sir."

He was still staring at her, eyes narrowed slightly. "On Friday."

"Yes, sir."

"During the shareholder's meeting?"

She had his full attention now and she felt oddly warm, and very uncomfortable, feeling the weight of his scrutiny. "I've found a replacement," she said, her voice cracking, her composure cracking. "She's highly qualified, shorthand, word processing, data processing—"

"No. Sorry," he cut her mercilessly off. "Reimburse yourself for the ticket from petty cash and leave me a copy of the ticket voucher."

Mr. Grady picked up the phone again and rapidly dialed a new number. Clearly he was done talking. "And those faxes, *Winnie*, you'll see to those immediately?"

Morgan Grady watched the rigid lines of Winnie Graham's back as she marched from his office, her sensible one-inch black heels clicking across his floor, her dark glasses sliding low on her nose.

"Shut the door, if you would," he added pleasantly, picking up the phone again.

She reached for the doorknob and her brown tweedy blazer gaped, exposing her severe cream blouse with the wing collar. The tweedy blazer wasn't appropriate for the heavy heat of June, and the cream blouse didn't flatter her complexion, but then, nothing she wore was fashionable and that suited him just fine. Work was work. Pleasure was pleasure. The lines never crossed.

Yet he couldn't help noting a faint tremor in her hand and he'd have to be a moron to not recognize that she was upset.

Well, that made two of them.

He knew exactly why she wanted the day off Friday and it made him madder than hell.

Miss Graham, his quiet unassuming Miss Graham had an interview scheduled on Friday in South Carolina.

His assistant was looking for another job when she was needed here. When *he* needed her here.

The press were digging into his past, looking for tidbits as if it were King Tut's tomb. They were making calls, investigating leads, trying to find out if Morgan Grady was really the fairy-tale story he appeared to be.

Morgan smiled grimly. Fairy-tale life? Hardly. But the details of his past belonged to him and even now, twenty-five years after being adopted, he still knew the stigma that came with being from Roxbury instead of Beacon Hill.

The Gradys were saints, he thought, swallowing hard. They'd known from the beginning who he was, where he came from, and they'd taken him in anyway. They'd made him one of them. Gave him their name, their love, their security, and it had been wonderful, but now the spotlight was intensifying and the heat was becoming unbearable. It wasn't that he was ashamed of his past, but he didn't want Big Mike to take any credit, or get the attention, or savor his son's success.

The only way to juggle the pressure of personal and professional was to keep a tight rein on his emotions, to remain focused, to stay on schedule.

And no one but no one was better than Winnie Graham at keeping him on task.

She knew her job. She was the best damn secretary he'd had in years, and after going through a half dozen in less than a year, he'd like to keep her, thank you very much.

Morgan stared at the closed door for a moment, remembering the pinched expression at Miss Graham's mouth and briefly considered calling her back in.

But what would he say then? *I know you're job hunting and I don't want you to leave?* Absolutely not.

He was the boss. She was the executive assistant. He made the decisions. She implemented them.

Impatiently he reached for the phone, placed another call, feeling the intense pressure he'd been under for months. In the last year his business had skyrocketed. Work was nothing short of insane. The sheer volume, and value of the deals, staggered him.

Winnie Graham couldn't leave. He needed her. Depended on her. Give Miss Graham Friday off? Not a chance.

Back at her desk, face still burning, Winnie numbly copied and faxed the documents Mr. Grady gave her before swiftly sorting through the afternoon's e-mails accumulating in her in-box.

She worked on automatic pilot, answering the most urgent e-mails, forwarding what was necessary and printing out the spreadsheets required even as her mind raced.

She couldn't, wouldn't, miss the job interview.

She could go back in and argue about leave time again, or she could just not show up Friday morning. It wasn't as if Mr. Grady didn't have other secretaries on the staff able to cover for her. Grady Investments was made up of a team of seventeen, which included the two assistants for the research analysts and the two assistants for the traders.

She was not essential on Friday. Any one of the other assistants could take notes, pour coffee, and smile grimly. Although the other secretaries would probably be delighted to assist Mr. Grady, she reflected, gritting her teeth in disgust. Everybody loved Mr. Grady.

Including her.

There, the truth. She'd admitted it at last. The reason she couldn't stay: Winnie couldn't bear having her heart stepped on anymore. It was time to get smart. Time to think about self-preservation.

Winnie's head began to pound and her stomach chose that moment to rumble. She'd just started a new diet— her third attempt this summer—and she still hadn't gotten used to working from lunch to dinner without the midafternoon cookie or candy bar. What she needed was some fresh air and something cold to drink.

Winnie reached into her top right desk drawer and scooped out her wallet before taking the elevator to the forty-second floor, and changed to the express elevator that whisked her to lobby level in less than ten seconds. It was a drastic free-for-all in her tummy and she swallowed hard when the elevators slid open a second time.

Life with Morgan Grady was a bit like riding the Tower elevators: a giddy ride up and down but nothing solid in between.

Yet after six months of wild rides, she was ready to get off.

She wanted a job with decent hours, solid benefits, and an elderly boring boss so she could sleep again at night.

Outside, Winnie drew a short breath, momentarily blindsided by the heat and noise. As she walked to the hot dog vendor on the corner, a truck roared past, followed by a dozen streaking yellow cabs, half leaning on their horns.

Winnie bought a can of icy soda and popped the top on her way back to the Tower's entrance. It was mid-afternoon and Manhattan's skyscrapers had already reduced the light into little grids of sun and shadow on the sidewalk.

When she announced she was moving to New York to work, her family had predicted she wouldn't survive a month. Instead she'd lasted over four years.

She didn't particularly want to leave Manhattan now, but she needed distance from Morgan and all her impossible, outrageous fantasies. At night she dreamed of him over and over and it only made reality worse.

Morgan Grady would never go for her. He dated socialites, models and actresses. Not pudgy secretaries who stuttered when nervous.

The Tower's revolving glass door turned and a woman Winnie only knew as Tiffany, joined her on the sidewalk in front of the building.

"It's that time of day," Tiffany said, tapping out a

cigarette and lighting up. She was tall, slender, with lots of blond highlights in her hair. She looked like the type that had tried to model in high school. "Just three more hours."

Winnie felt a stab of envy. "You go home at five?"

"Most of the time. If I'm lucky." Tiffany dragged on the cigarette and exhaled. She cast Winnie a bored glance. "Where do you work?"

"On the seventy-eighth floor."

"The seventy-eighth?" Tiffany's eyebrows arched, her interest piqued. "Then you must work for Grady Investments."

Suddenly Winnie didn't feel like talking anymore. Women always wanted to be friends with her if they thought it'd get them closer to Morgan Grady. "Yes," she answered, voice clipped.

"So what's he like?" Tiffany persisted.

Winnie pushed her glasses higher on the bridge of her nose. "Who?"

Tiffany let out a little laugh, her pink-painted lips parted. "Very funny. Morgan Grady, silly. You work in his office. You must have met him. What's he like…I mean, really, what's he *like?*"

"Busy."

"Of course. He's huge. He completely dominates the investment world. Everyone pays attention to his market forecasts."

Winnie forced a small, tight smile. "Isn't that nice?"

"But the part I find most amazing, is that he's not just this brilliant brain in a glass jar—he's gorgeous, too." Tiffany sounded positively giddy. "No wonder he's been named New York's Sexiest Bachelor twice in a row. He's sexier than sin. I'd kill for a moment alone with him."

"And I should just kill myself," Winnie muttered beneath her breath, feeling painfully inadequate. Living on the periphery of Morgan Grady's world was about as excruciating a thing as Winnie had ever experienced.

Thank God she'd soon be working somewhere else. Maybe then she'd get some self-esteem back.

Tiffany had a one-track mind. "What's he like as a boss?"

"Let me loan you my book, *Never Work for a Jerk,* and then you tell me what you think."

Tiffany giggled. "Is there really such a book?"

"Yes."

Tiffany laughed even harder. "And you have a copy?"

"No, not yet. But I plan on buying it soon."

Tiffany was laughing so hard she had to wipe her eyes. "I had no idea you were so funny," she cried, tapping her cigarette. "Who would have thought?"

"Yes, who would have thought?" A voice coolly cut in. It was a deep voice, husky and distinctly male, a voice Winnie knew far too well. "She's a woman of many hidden talents."

Winnie felt ice water flood her limbs. *Mr. Grady!*

"And her next job," he continued dryly, "will be working as a standup comedian."

CHAPTER THREE

IT COULDN'T be. He couldn't be here. He didn't hear her say that...did he?

Paling, Winnie turned to discover Morgan Grady behind her, a black trench coat thrown over his arm, his long dark hair almost tidy.

"Mr. Grady," she whispered, her mouth drying. "Heading out?"

He gazed down at her, his expression curiously hard. "I've been trying to reach you."

Heat surged to her cheeks. "I came down for a soda."

"I see."

There was a moment of strained silence between them, something that had never happened before. He'd always talked; she'd always listened. He'd never been silent with her before. "Did you want something?"

"You had a phone call from a Mrs. Fielding. She said it was urgent. I left the number on your desk."

Winnie couldn't remember Mrs. Fielding and wondered what could possibly be urgent. "Thank you."

His dense black lashes lowered, his mouth compressed. "Next time you might want to remember to take this," he added, extending his arm to reveal her small pager.

Winnie moved to take the pager from him but tensed

as her fingers brushed his palm and a sharp current of sensation sizzled through her.

He was angry.

In her five and a half months with him he'd never displayed any emotion and yet now he was angry.

Quickly, to hide her confusion, Winnie clipped the pager to the waistband of her skirt even as Tiffany dropped her cigarette, stubbing it out with the spike of her high heel.

"Mr. Grady," Tiffany murmured, her voice dropping an octave as she held out her hand.

He hesitated, turned ever so slightly, and smiled a cool quizzical smile. It was a smile he must have practiced for moments like this, when he needed to put distance between himself and others without appearing aloof. The smile was a little slow, a little crooked, and made his rugged jaw wider, his cheekbones stronger. "We've met?"

"Once," Tiffany answered archly. Her smile stretched as his hand closed around hers, her cheeks glowing with the faintest touch of pink. "Well, we sort of met. You had business with one of the firm's partners and I notarized the paperwork."

"Ah." Morgan's teeth had never looked so straight or white and he continued to hold her hand in his. "You work with Jeff."

"Yes. He thinks the world of you. We all do."

A black limousine slid next to the curb, and the driver shifted into neutral but the car remained on, engine idling. Morgan Grady released Tiffany's hand, glanced at the limo, and then back at Tiffany. "I must run, but it was a pleasure meeting you, Miss—"

"Saunders. Tiffany Saunders. And I work with Jeff."

"On the sixty-third floor, right." He smiled again, and Winnie could see why women melted at his feet. There was something in his eyes, something in his energy and intensity that made you feel—however brief— that you were special. That you were the only one alive.

Winnie sucked in a painful, self-conscious breath.

He'd never looked at her once that way.

He'd never even gotten her name right.

A lump filled her throat and Winnie wished with all her heart she'd never worked for Morgan Grady.

Mr. Grady started for the waiting car, conversation forgotten, no goodbyes necessary. Move On, seemed to be his unwritten motto, no time to linger, no patience for niceties. Just move on to the next thing on the agenda.

But suddenly he stopped and turned back. It was muggy hot, the muggy hot of New York in late June when the air felt thick and yellow, yet he looked coolly elegant in his black suit and shirt.

She wondered how he did it, how he handled the heat and pressure without sweating or wilting or fading.

How did he predict the market before the market knew what it was going to do?

How did he juggle dozens of complicated, million and billion dollar deals without worrying, panicking, overeating?

She didn't know. She couldn't know. He was nothing like her.

Mr. Grady was staring at her now, his high tanned brow slightly furrowed. "Are you job hunting, Miss Graham?"

It was the last question she expected from him, the absolutely last thing she expected him to say, and Winnie wobbled in her sensible heels.

She reached for a handkerchief from her pocket and came up with nothing. Instead she gripped the pager in her perspiring hand. Good Lord. Did he know about her job interview, too? Or was it just a joke, a follow-up to his comedian remark moments ago?

Winnie blinked, swallowed, and blinked again, her glasses fogging slightly, her thoughts spinning in no logical direction.

What was she supposed to say? How was she supposed to answer that?

"No," she blurted at last, cheeks darkening. "Of course not."

His eyebrows lifted. He stared at her hard, his lips twisting ever so slightly.

Her blush deepened. She felt like a willful child with a hand caught in the cookie jar.

"Of course not," he echoed softly, mockery in his voice. "I'll see you later," he said.

"Right."

Then he turned away and climbed into the back of the waiting limousine.

Tiffany silently disappeared into the lobby of the Tower's building leaving Winnie alone on the sidewalk.

For a long moment Winnie didn't move, her heart thumping hard and fast. What had just happened out here? What did Mr. Grady mean?

Finally she shook off her fear, threw away her lukewarm soda and returned upstairs.

Winnie worked until dinner and then when she'd

done all she could for the day, turned off her computer and took the subway home.

She was back at the office the next morning at six-thirty. As usual she was the first of the administrative assistants to arrive and Winnie made it her job every morning to turn on the office lights, check the thermostat and get the coffee brewing.

Coffee percolating, Winnie left the employee break room and headed toward the back office suite, flicking on lights as she went.

She arrived at Mr. Grady's office and froze.

Mr. Grady was already in, he was sitting at his desk, and his door was ajar. He never left his door ajar. He was a man that preferred privacy always.

She stood there, transfixed, listening to him type, his fingers tapping away at his computer keyboard.

Something was wrong. The door shouldn't be open. He shouldn't be at his computer yet. He should still be reading his papers.

What had happened? Was it something to do with the press? She'd had three calls yesterday from various media sources, or was this more personal? Did this have anything to do with…her?

The tapping on the keyboard briefly stopped and Winnie felt the strangest, most physical sensation shoot through her. She could *feel* him.

Her brain told her that he hadn't left his desk but her body was reacting totally different. The fine hair on her nape rose. Her skin prickled. Her body felt incredibly sensitive all over.

She'd never been so keenly aware of him before. It

was almost as if he was standing right here next to her, touching her.

Heat banded across her cheekbones. She drew a slow breath. She was being overly dramatic, she lectured herself, forcing herself to action.

Winnie headed for her desk, took off her lightweight trench coat and hung it on the hook next to the filing cabinet before moving to her desk.

As she rolled out her chair she spotted a book with a lime green cover lying in the middle of her desk.

She didn't remember leaving a book on her desk last night. She always left her desk clean, virtually spotless.

She moved closer, lifted the book. *Never Work for a Jerk.*

She dropped the book as if she'd been burned. Good God. The book. It was *the* book. The book she'd mentioned to Tiffany. He'd gone out and bought her a copy.

Winnie sagged into her chair, sitting down in a heavy heap, her purse falling to her feet.

He was going to fire her. That's why his door was ajar. He was waiting for her to get here so he could give her the ax.

It wasn't supposed to go like this. She'd been the one looking for a new job. She'd been the one hurt. It was her feelings that had been trampled.

And yet had he ever badmouthed her? Had he ever publicly insulted her? Had he ever insulted her even in private?

Why had she said what she'd said to Tiffany? Why had she let her emotions get the better of her? What was the saying? Open mouth, insert foot?

Well, it was more like, open mouth, insert body.

She felt really, deeply embarrassed.

The small intercom on her desk made a faint clicking sound. "Miss Graham, when you've a minute, I'd like to see you."

Her heart jumped. She couldn't make herself move, unable to find enough strength in her legs.

But she couldn't ignore him. She was already in trouble. She might as well get this over with, go face the firing squad.

Winnie rolled away from her desk and stood up, pressing her blue pleated skirt smooth, making sure every pleat fell straight. It was her smartest skirt, the one she wore when she needed to feel extra crisp, extra professional. If ever there was a day she needed it, it was now.

The intercom clicked again. "Oh, and Miss Graham, you don't need to bring the book with you."

Morgan watched Winnie enter his office, her eyes wide behind her dark glasses, the black frames resting halfway down her straight nose. She sat down gingerly on the edge of the chair that faced his desk and folded her hands across the notebook and pen she'd brought with her.

He struggled to be civil. "Good morning."

"Good morning, Mr. Grady."

He leaned back in his swivel chair. "How are you?"

Her lashes fluttered behind the lenses of her glasses. Her lashes were long and they brushed the glass. "I'm fine, thank you."

Her voice sounded firm, decisive, every inch the competent secretary he'd been relying upon these past six months.

She swallowed hard. "About the book—"

"I don't want to discuss the book."

A pulse had begun to beat rapidly at the base of her throat. "You don't?"

"No. I knew you wanted it, so I bought a copy for you. Happy Secretaries Day."

"That was back in April, Mr. Grady."

"Better late than never." He sat forward, touched a button on his keyboard and checked the European market before it closed. His gaze skimmed the various stock prices before sitting back again.

"I have to be able to trust my staff," he said after a moment, grateful his voice could sound so calm when he didn't feel the least bit calm, and hadn't since overhearing her flippant remark yesterday in front of the office building.

His perfect secretary was a fraud.

Until now he'd thought of her as a future Miss Robinson, Miss Robinson being his first executive assistant and hands down, the best. Miss Robinson was tidy, precise, efficient, intelligent, controlled. She was always one step ahead of him and practically anticipated his every need before he even knew the need himself.

Miss Robinson had been with him for seven years, and retired eighteen months ago, just before he bought out Bradley Finance in a friendly acquisition. Trying to fill Miss Robinson's shoes had been impossible and he'd gone through assistant after assistant until he inherited Winnie Graham through the Bradley acquisition.

He hadn't thought he'd like Miss Graham, hadn't expected anyone who hid behind large dark glasses and a mass of pinned-up braids to be as effective as his esteemed Miss Robinson but Winnie Graham wasn't just good. She was great. She was the future Miss Robinson, the superlative secretary who knew what he wanted before he even wanted it.

"I need to trust you," he said. "You have complete access to me. You know details about my personal life, my family, my finances. If you're going to talk to Tiffany from the sixty-third floor, what's to say you won't talk to a friendly reporter?"

Her head lifted and her unblinking gaze met his. He watched as she adjusted her glasses. "Because I won't," she answered crisply.

"But you did yesterday—"

"And it was a mistake!" She rose from her chair. She'd never interrupted him before, never contradicted him and her passionate response surprised both of them. "I'm sorry, Mr. Grady, I feel terrible about what happened yesterday. It was careless of me, but I honestly didn't mean anything by it—"

"Are you looking for a new job?"

Her lips parted and color seared her cheeks but no sound came from her mouth.

She didn't answer because she couldn't answer, he thought, rocking forward in his chair, reaching for his phone, needing something, anything to do to keep his temper in check.

How had this happened? Where had he misjudged her?

"Never mind," he uttered shortly, unable to remember the last time he felt so cheated, or deceived. "I know you want Friday off. Take it off."

Winnie sank back into her seat. "Please forgive me,"

she whispered, cheeks stained red, fingers kneading in her lap. "I admire you so much. I think the world of you."

"It didn't sound like that yesterday."

"I know, but it's not why you think." Her fingers tightened together. "Tiffany was gushing. Everyone gushes and…" She took a deep breath. "I don't want to sound like one of them. I wanted to be…cool."

"Cool?"

"Cool," she repeated shakily. "I've never been cool in my life and women are always asking about you, beautiful glamorous women, and I get insecure. I can't believe I'm even telling you this but it's true. I'm a geek. I just wanted Tiffany to think I was like her."

"Like her?"

"You know, sophisticated."

He hadn't heard anything so pitiful in years. His incredibly intelligent and capable assistant wanted to impress a ditzy airhead like Tiffany? *Why?*

He stared at Winnie hard, trying to see past the glasses and firm press of her lips and what he saw was a young oval face with a high, pale forehead and small rounded chin.

"You have my approval," he said after a moment. "Why do you need hers?"

She didn't move a muscle. Her fixed expression didn't change. Her stillness coupled with the heightened color in her cheeks reminded him of a painting, an oil portrait from the turn of the century.

"That's a good question, sir."

"Think about it," he said, frustrated, angry and not at all sure what to do. Should he fire her? Could he trust her? What was supposed to happen next? "Are you going to a job interview on Friday?"

She hesitated for the briefest moment. "Yes."

He was out of patience. Sitting forward, Morgan punched another button on his market monitor. The market was open. Trading had begun. "If you take the job, I'll expect two weeks' notice."

Winnie looked away, stared past his shoulder to the wall of windows behind him. There was no emotion in her face. She looked like the serene, capable assistant he'd always known. "How did you find out about my job interview?"

His stomach felt hard, tight. He hated conflict. Hated feeling mistrustful. Charlotte had done a number on him, and while it'd been fifteen years since she betrayed him, some things were impossible to forget.

But Morgan didn't let any of his emotion show. He'd learned years ago to keep his personal life private. "Mr. Osborne's office called on Monday doing a reference check. I spoke with Mr. Osborne personally."

Winnie's head lifted, and her gaze met his, eyes large and worried behind the heavy glasses. "What did you say?"

He felt his lips twist into a ghost of a smile. "That you were the best damn secretary I'd ever had."

"Morgan, we're worried about you. Reed's worried about you." Rose Grady's precise diction was even more vigorous than usual. "Every time we turn on the television, you're there. We can't pick up a magazine without a story about you."

Morgan finished pulling his T-shirt over his head,

having stripped off his suit and changed into jeans and a T-shirt now that he was home.

"You're sick of my press?" he teased, shifting the phone from one ear to the other as he headed for the kitchen.

"That's not what I mean," Rose retorted indignantly and Morgan could picture the elegant arch of her eyebrows rising higher. "We know how hard you've worked at putting the past behind you, but now these reporters are digging into everything. And I do mean, *everything*."

Morgan popped open the mineral water and took a long cool drink. "It's going to be all right," he said, wanting to believe his own optimism as he leaned against a stainless-steel counter, his kitchen huge and modern, big enough to accommodate a fleet of chefs. "The reporters will hound someone else soon. People get bored and move on."

"That's not all, Morgan. There's something else, and I'm not sure how to tell you, or even if I should tell you, but I don't want you to hear this from anyone else."

"Then tell me."

Silence stretched across the line. "I saw Charlotte."

Morgan froze. *"What?"*

"Charlotte came to the house."

It felt as if he'd been slammed on the chest with a shovel. He couldn't catch his breath. "Alone?"

"Yes."

He set the water down so forcefully the bottle rattled on the counter. "What did she want?"

"To hear about you. To know what you've been doing all these years."

Charlotte. *Charlotte*. "What did you tell her?"

Rose sighed impatiently. "I said, read the papers. Turn on the evening news. Morgan's life is everywhere."

He nearly smiled. Trust Rose to give an answer like that.

"She says, she made a mistake," Rose continued more faintly, as if delivering this information caused her great pain. "She indicated she wanted to make amends."

"It's been fifteen years."

"You once wanted this."

"Fifteen years ago."

"Five years ago," Rose rebutted.

Morgan shook his head slowly, angrily, not understanding why this had to happen now when he had so much pressure on him, when he had so many people depending on him. "How did she look?"

"Even more beautiful. She's certainly matured well. She's a classic beauty. What do you expect?"

His chest tightened. He closed his eyes. He didn't want to hear this, didn't want to know this. "I don't want to talk to her."

"Fine."

"And I don't want to see her."

"Then don't."

But even as he said the words, he was laughing at himself. Who was he kidding? Even fifteen years after she disappeared from his life he still wasn't over her.

"Rose...Mom.."Morgan pressed a clenched fist to

his forehead, battling fears that very few knew about. "What do I do? How do I get out of this?"

"First of all, forget Charlotte, she's inconsequential," Rose said crisply, comfortable taking charge again. "And second, get rid of the press!"

"How?"

"Morgan, you're smart. Throw them a bone. Give the media a story…and I don't mean Charlotte!"

CHAPTER FOUR

RIDING the subway to work the next morning, Winnie heard Mr. Grady's words ring in her head. *The best damn secretary he'd ever had.* It was the highest compliment she could be paid. It was the highest compliment she'd ever been paid, and as pitiful as it sounded, those words from Mr. Grady meant everything to her.

She shifted on the subway seat, already sticky and warm despite the air-conditioning. Winnie told herself it was the summer heat wave making her feel a little hot, and more than a little bit crazy, but really, it had less to do with the thermometer than it did with her own feelings.

Two days from now and she'd be on a plane for the final interview in Charleston and she dreaded the interview now in Charleston, she dreaded her last day at Grady Investments, she dreaded everything to do with leaving.

Don't think about it, she told herself, as the subway arrived at her stop and she lurched to her feet. You have two weeks before you have to say goodbye. No reason to cross that bridge today.

The advice had been sound, but the moment Mr. Grady walked into the office, Winnie's heart did the same wild lurch it always did, making her feel as if she were on the subway or elevator again.

What was it about him that she loved so much? She

stared at his eyes, his mouth, his chin and while the
features were all perfectly shaped, her interest had less
to do with the physical perfection than the intensity beneath.

There was something about him, she thought, putting
the top of her pen to her mouth, something deeper, more
complex than he wanted to reveal. But what?

"Good morning, Winnie."

"Good morning, Mr. Grady." She managed a firm,
professional smile. It was the competent smile she knew
executives preferred. "The president of Shipley's Bank
just called. Would you like me to get him back on the
line?"

"Not just yet. I have a couple of things to take care
of first. I'll let you know when I'm ready."

"Of course, Mr. Grady. Is there anything else I can
do for you right now?"

"No. Just hold all calls."

"Yes, Mr. Grady. I'll do that, Mr. Grady."

His door closed and she sank back into her chair and
covered her face with her hands. Could she possibly
sound more pathetic? *Mr. Grady. No, Mr. Grady. Isn't
the sky perfectly blue, Mr. Grady?*

She sounded like a simpering idiot. *Winnie, you need
a life.*

You need to be good at something besides typing.
You need to have interests other than Morgan Grady.
You need to stop waiting for something good to happen.

And suddenly tears filled her eyes, ridiculous tears
that had nothing to do with work and everything to do
with wanting so much and not knowing how to accom-
plish any of it.

Once the tears started, she couldn't seem to make them stop. Suddenly she was crying because she was the middle daughter and the uninspiring daughter and the only one of her sisters who wasn't spectacular. Alexis and Megan were stunning, and talented, and incredibly popular. Unlike Winnie who'd never even been invited to the prom, Alexis and Megan had never missed a high school dance.

She'd never been beautiful or special, and as horrible as the tears were, as embarrassing as they were, they were real. It's hard to be plain and unexciting when the world embraces style and beauty.

The tears continued to stream and Winnie, who firmly believed that tears didn't belong at the office, grabbed a tissue from the box of Kleenex and blew her nose before being forced to pull off her glasses and wipe her eyes dry.

"Are you all right?" It was Mr. Grady, and his voice was coming from above her desk. She hadn't heard his door open or his footsteps approach.

Winnie struggled to hide the tears and quickly tossed the damp tissue away. "Yes, Mr. Grady. I'm just great."

His skeptical gaze swept her face. She knew she was a wreck when she cried. Some women were delicate weepers. She was not. Her nose went shiny. Her eyes turned pink. Her complexion took on a mottled hue. But she squeezed her lips into a smile and prayed it'd work.

It didn't. His brow creased deeper. "You look like you're in agony. Do you want to go home? Take an early lunch?"

"Heavens, no. It's not even nine-thirty, sir, and it's nothing…it's just…it's just…"

"Just what?"

"I've made a mistake."

"I'm sure it can be fixed."

"No, it's too late."

"Is it a stock order? A market transaction?" he asked, clearly dumbfounded.

"No, it's about my job. This job, and the job in Charleston. I don't know what I'm supposed to do anymore. I don't know what's right anymore—" She broke off, eyes welling up again, and Winnie struggled to get her glasses back on, but in her haste she bypassed one ear and the black frames ended up dangling off her face.

"I think you've missed something," Morgan said surprisingly gently.

"An ear, sir." She hiccuped, took the glasses off, and slid them on correctly, hooking the glasses around each ear with as much composure as she could muster considering the fact that her nose had gone stuffy and her voice sounded thick and she'd just been sobbing her heart out. She wasn't making sense. She knew she wasn't making sense and it only made her feel worse.

"I'm sorry," she said, drawing a deep breath, trying to calm herself. "I'm fine now. I just had something in my eye—"

"I think those are called tears, Winnie."

She smiled faintly at his joke. It was a feeble joke but she appreciated it. "Yes, you're right. And I'm fine now. Please, go back to work and put this out of mind."

"Easier said than done."

"It's an achievable goal, sir." She turned to face her

computer, her fingers hovering above her keyboard and fixing her gaze on her computer screen she waited for him to disappear.

He did not. He remained where he stood, just across her desk, his tall, solid body a delight in Italian wool and Egyptian cotton. She could smell his fragrance, smell the tantalizing hint of musk, and her gaze slowly lifted, traveling up his white shirt, past the elegant gray and black tie to the square cut of his chin and his impressive lips. She thought sometimes she'd do just about anything to have a kiss from those lips...

And there she went again, fantasizing, like she'd spent half the night last night.

Last night she'd imagined driving around Manhattan in the back of Morgan's black stretch limo and she was wearing something silky and clingy and they were kissing madly. His hand was cupping her breast and she was making desperate little whimpering sounds and she couldn't get enough of his mouth, of his hands. In her dream she wasn't stodgy old Winnie, but someone exciting, someone smart and funny and beautiful. But of course morning came and she woke and dragged herself into the bathroom for a reality-check shower.

And still he stood there, before her desk. She didn't know what he wanted, what he was waiting for. Winnie dropped her hands back into her lap. "Do you need something, Mr. Grady?"

He was looking at her most strangely. Looking at her as if she wasn't Winnie but someone else. The slash of his black eyebrows drew closer together and a lock of dark hair fell forward on his brow. "Yes. I want to know more about the job in Charleston. Why were you interested in it?''

Heat filled her, a warm slow heat that made her tingle from head to toe. She knew what she was, and saw herself all too clearly—slightly pudgy, rather frumpy, and prone to panic attacks—but oh, how she loved him and oh, how she wanted him. But living in fantasyland was just about to do her in.

''Change,'' she answered huskily, wishing yet again she were someone else, someone with style, someone with grace, someone that men would fight to ask out. Although, really, she didn't want *men,* she wanted just one man. Morgan.

What a stupid, futile wish. What a stupid, futile path she was traveling.

Sniffling, she jerked open her desk drawer and dug around for a paper clip to stop her eyes from welling yet again. She had to get a grip. She had to get on with things. Because even if she wore a red dress and put hot rollers in her hair, she wasn't the supermodel of Morgan Grady's world. Wake up, Winnie. Grow up, Winnie. You're never going to be his type.

''But you like New York?'' he persisted.

She swallowed the lump in her throat. Of course she liked New York. *He* lived in New York. She'd love Timbuktu if that's where he was. ''Yes, Mr. Grady.''

''So the problem is here, at the office.''

Her chest felt raw, her lungs ached with bottled air. ''Yes.''

His black eyebrows drew even more tightly together. ''You don't like working for me?''

Like didn't exactly factor into it. It was more of a

love-hate thing. She loved working for him but hated being a nobody. She didn't want to be his secretary. She was dying to be his lover.

Winnie bent her head, rolled her eyes. How perfectly Ninny Winnie.

"So it is me," Morgan repeated.

"No!" She looked up at him, emotion so strong she was sure he could see what she was feeling in her eyes. But she did need to tell him something because obviously, she was having a problem right now. Her job search. The book on her desk. Her emotional breakdown just now. This wasn't the dependable, rational Winnie Graham he knew. She wasn't exactly a rock this week.

"It's not you," she said hoarsely, ashamed that she was practically disintegrating again. "It's me."

He shook his head, lines fanning from his eyes, deep grooves etched beside his mouth. "I don't understand."

Her eyes burned and she fought the urge to sniffle. She knew her nose must be bright red and her glasses were fogging up. "I've fallen in love."

There was a moment of dead silence and then a small muscle in his jaw popped. "With someone here? At Grady Investments?"

He couldn't have sounded more incredulous. "Yes."

It wasn't a lie. She had fallen in love and she was in a muddle and she'd never been so emotional in all her life.

He leaned on her desk, leaned so close to her she caught another hint of spice. "He doesn't love you?"

Her eyes burned and she swallowed hard. "Oh, no, sir. He's not interested in me."

"Is he married?"

She shook her had swiftly. "No."

"Has he taken advantage of you?"

She couldn't help blushing. "No. No, it's not like that. The problem is, he doesn't know I exist while I...I—"

"You what?"

"I'm crazy about him." She averted her head, wishing she could just crawl into some city manhole and hide. "Hopelessly crazy."

"That does sound bad."

"It is," she answered huskily, her voice breaking. She could feel his gaze rest on her, felt what seemed to be sympathy, and she didn't want it from him. "Which is why I started looking for a new job. I knew this wasn't working out and I thought change was necessary. I thought it'd be wise to put some distance between us."

Mr. Grady looked troubled. "But if he doesn't know...?"

"It doesn't matter if he knows or not, *I know.* I know when he's here. I listen for his footsteps, for his voice, for everything." She bit her lip, fought for control. "But it's too painful. I can't do this anymore."

He studied her for a long silent moment and then shook his head. "Fine. Tell me his name and I'll fire him."

Winnie nearly fell off her chair. "Mr. Grady!"

"I'm not going to let one of my most valuable staff members ruin her career."

"You can't blame him!"

"I don't. But I'm also not going to stand by and watch you walk out because some guy here is knocking around your heart. If you can't stand coming to work because Mr. Heartbreak works here, then give me his name and let's get this over with.''

She couldn't believe he was serious. He'd fire someone because she wasn't happy here anymore? "You can't be serious."

"He'll get an excellent severance package."

"Mr. Grady!"

"And the best references."

"No."

"I want his name."

"No." Her phone rang and she looked at the handset where the number and name of the caller flashed. "It's Shipley's Bank again," she said, heart hammering, hands shaking and yet incredibly grateful for the interruption.

"His name, Winnie."

Her phone rang again. She tensed, muscles tightening everywhere. When the phone rang a third time she couldn't keep silent. "I'm going to answer. Do you want to take the call or should I take a message?"

He didn't say a word, his dark blue gaze locked with hers. He didn't look angry as much as determined, jaw jutted, expression intense.

Winnie reached for the phone, "Mr. Grady's office, may I help you?"

He gave his head a slow shake and mouthed the words, "This isn't over, Winnie," before returning to his office.

He remained sequestered in his office on the call with Shipley's Bank for nearly two hours before leaving directly for a meeting across town.

After he left, Winnie let out a long sigh of relief. She'd been sitting on pins and needles the past two hours and wanted nothing more than to get a break herself. She opted for a rare luxury—lunch out, heading down the street to her favorite deli two blocks away.

But not even a lunch out could erase her worry. Business and pleasure didn't mix. Careers were destroyed over office romances. It'd be disastrous for her to remain at Grady Investments much longer. She felt it in every bone of her body.

Winnie walked slowly back to the Tower's building, trying to ignore her reflection in the mirror-glass building fronts but it was impossible to deny the black glasses, beige blouse, hair scraped back from her face which screamed, uptight. Make that uptight, unsatisfied *virgin.*

Yes, an uptight, unsatisfied virgin. That's exactly what she'd become.

Winnie stopped and stared at her reflection and hated what she saw. This wasn't her. This isn't how she felt on the inside. On the inside she was madly passionate, daring beyond measure. On the inside she wanted everything and was willing to risk all—

On the inside.

There lay the problem. No one knew about Winnie on the inside. No one saw the fun side, or adventurous side of her. No, she kept that side buttoned down and pressed back because once upon a time she decided if she wasn't going to be popular and sexy and fashionable then she damn well better get respect.

Respect. Augh! Respect was fine for seventy-year-old

matriarchs, but she was twenty-five. She had no social life. No dates. No romance.

No wonder.

Impatiently Winnie reached up and undid the top button of her stiff blouse. She didn't want to be uptight. She didn't want to be unsatisfied. She didn't want to go through life without ever experiencing anything.

Winnie unbuttoned the next button. Checked her reflection again. Still boring, still a virgin, still really really not sexy.

And let's face it, two buttons unfastened on a beige blouse were not exactly a makeover. What she needed was a miracle. What she wanted was a life-changing experience.

She'd give up everything, she thought, if for one week—no, make that a month—she could look like Tiffany from the sixty-third floor. Sexy, curvy, sensual. A woman that made men hot. A woman that made men melt.

Crossing the lobby Winnie's sensible heels clicked loudly on the floor. She pressed the elevator up button and waited. A moment later the elevator doors opened. People streamed out. Winnie stepped back to let the others pass. As she moved out of the way, Tiffany Saunders grabbed Winnie's arm.

"Hey," Tiffany cried, latching onto Winnie's sleeve as if they were life-long friends. "I just heard the news. It must be nuts upstairs!"

"What news?"

"About Morgan Grady. *News Weekly*'s Man of the Year. Isn't it incredible?"

Winnie blinked blankly. "But Mr. Morgan isn't Man of the Year, he was Sexiest Man—"

"No, no. This just happened. The magazine doesn't hit the stands until tomorrow but it was announced on the noon news broadcast today. The media are everywhere. They're swarming upstairs—" Tiffany broke off, eyes widening. "You didn't know? Where've you been?"

Winnie's throat dried. "Out to lunch."

"Well, honey, you better check in because your Morgan Grady is Man of the Year."

The express elevator to the seventy-eighth floor always left Winnie's stomach at her feet, and today was worse than ever.

Stepping off the elevator, she walked into a frenzied sea of reporters and carefully picked her way through the crowd to the reception desk. The young receptionist at the front desk, flagged Winnie down. "Thank God you're here," the receptionist choked. "They won't go away and they just keep arriving and I don't know what to do."

"They're here for Mr. Grady?"

"Yes. It's about the Man of the Year award. The phones keep ringing—" She was interrupted by the telephone and her face crumpled as she sat down again to take the call.

Winnie sized up the crowd. Tiffany was right. It was bedlam in here. Every reporter from every paper and TV station must have a representative in the reception area.

Poor Mr. Grady.

The receptionist hung up the phone. "So what do I do, Winnie? How do I get rid of them?"

"Tell them he's not here."

"I did, but they don't care. They won't leave. They want Mr. Grady and they're going to stay until he arrives."

Winnie recognized the stricken look on the poor girl's face and her conscience pricked her. She couldn't leave this eighteen-year-old from Nebraska to deal with this snapping, yapping throng. The journalists had been kept waiting for over an hour and they were impatient, hungry, and doing a very good imitation of a pack of wild dogs.

She also knew how Mr. Grady would hate returning to face this crowd. He'd never sought out the media, had never wanted to be a poster boy for the gorgeous and eligible. He routinely declined interviews, shunned society events, donated anonymously instead of funding charities publicly.

In the last six months she'd witnessed firsthand how the media hounded him. Board meetings, morning runs in Central Park, and dinner dates were nothing more than photo ops for the determined press.

Just last week a reporter with a microphone jumped out from a stall in the men's washroom in hopes of getting a good sound bite for the evening's news.

Morgan Grady was a hunted man.

Winnie felt a wave of loyalty, laced with pity. Facing the noisy throng she put two fingers in her mouth and whistled. The piercing sound silenced the crowd. "Thank you," Winnie said briskly. "Now is there something I can do for you all or are you here applying for a job?''

Winnie's question drew some reluctant laughs and the crowd jostled closer. ''Is Morgan Grady here?'' one reporter shouted above the rest.

''No, he is not,'' she answered.

''Where is he now?''

Winnie crossed her arms over her chest. ''In a conference across town.''

''Does he know he's been selected *News Weekly*'s Man of the Year?''

Winnie's eyebrows arched. ''What do you think?''

The crowd laughed again. Another reporter stepped forward. ''When do you expect him back?''

''Not until you're gone.''

And they laughed harder, real chuckles mixed with mock groans. Winnie couldn't help smiling back, realizing that some of the tension in the reception area had finally dissipated. For the first time in days she felt as though she'd finally done something right.

Just then, from the corner of her eye, she saw the elevator doors slide open and inside the gleaming paneled elevator stood Morgan Grady.

Her heart lurched.

His gaze met hers and held. Her smile faded and she felt the most intense longing for all the things she'd never had, for all the passion she'd never known.

What impossible desires, she thought, *what painful impossible dreams.*

She shook her head slightly, a nearly imperceptible shake that only Morgan noticed. *You don't want to get off here,* she tried to tell him. *You don't want to go through this now.*

Morgan remained inside the elevator and the doors slid soundlessly closed.

He'd escaped.

CHAPTER FIVE

HE'D escaped.

Morgan let himself into his Fifth Avenue apartment and shut the door behind him. A row of extravagant floral arrangements crowded the marble-topped eighteenth-century mahogany sideboard with dolphin feet. Those were new.

He scanned the florist envelopes, reluctant to open any of them. He could guess who'd sent the arrangements and he could imagine the sentiment expressed. It wasn't that he didn't appreciate the support—it was wonderful to have such a loving family—but he didn't feel celebratory.

How ironic that a big day like this should leave him cold. He hated the fuss. Didn't know how to internalize success like this.

The phone began to ring and Morgan started to move, but stopped as he heard Mr. Foley, butler and chef, answer it. Mr. Foley was taking a message, murmuring thanks and saying goodbye.

The phone rang almost immediately again, and then the doorbell chimed.

Morgan closed his eyes, pressed a fist to the middle of his forehead, and wished he were anywhere but here. Most people would have loved the honor *News Weekly* bestowed on him today, but it was the last thing Morgan needed. He couldn't bear to be the focus of so much attention. The hype reminded him too much of where he'd been.

The doorbell chimed a second time.

He had to get out of the limelight, had to do something soon. But first, the door.

Morgan opened the door, accepted an even more lavish bouquet, a huge crystal vase filled with lilies and orchids. There was no room left on the crowded table and Morgan set the vase down on the limestone floor.

Mr. Foley appeared in the doorway. He wore a dark suit, white shirt, dark tie, all very crisp and formal. "Congratulations, sir."

Morgan struggled to smile as he nodded his thanks but the smile never came. He hadn't felt this lonely in years. "Thank you, Mr. Foley."

The butler bowed. "Can I get you a drink, sir? A celebratory champagne, perhaps?"

"Gin and tonic is fine."

"Of course, sir. And congratulations again, sir."

No, lonely wasn't the right word, Morgan thought, correcting himself as he glanced around his expansive entry hall, teeming with flowers and the overpowering sweetness of lilies. He wasn't lonely. He felt alone. It was a subtle, but significant, difference.

It was a difference that continued to haunt him hours later as he lay in bed. How had he become this larger-than-life figure?

He wasn't a cool, sophisticated playboy, nor was he Wall Street's Boy Genius and he hated the cult of personality. The Morgan Grady the media glorified had never existed. He saw what they saw—Ivy League schools, gorgeous girlfriends, tremendous wealth. On paper, he looked good. In an Italian suit, he looked even better. But scratch a little at the surface polish, peek beneath the diplomas, the social life, the tailored suit, and he was Morgan O'Connell, Big Mike's terrified kid, a kid so desperate to escape his neighborhood that he took all kinds of jobs to get him off the street and away from the fighting.

He'd folded newspapers at four in the morning, delivered them on his bike at five, collected payments from the high-class neighborhoods in the afternoon.

When he'd finished delivering papers, he collected beer bottles and Coke cans, and then started mowing lawns. He'd made up flyers and pasted them on bulletin boards, stuck them in mailboxes, pushed them under people's doors.

Morgan O'Connell. Yardwork, Painting, Cleaning, Odd Jobs. Excellent work at cheap prices. References available. Will work after school and every weekend.

Anything for a buck.

Anything to escape the decrepit building called home.

Anything to avoid Big Mike's mean temper and quick fist.

Eyes burning, Morgan grabbed his pillow, and turned over on his stomach. The sheet slipped low on his hip, leaving his torso bare.

The Gradys helped him leave his old neighborhood behind, and he'd made enough bucks now to ensure financial security. But he still didn't feel as if he'd made it. And work, which had been his safest haven, had become a nightmare. How to do this? How to continue like this? How to be someone he wasn't?

Closing his eyes, he rested his cheek on the cool cotton pillowcase. But with his eyes closed he saw a dark shape, and the shape became a squiggly black-green tattoo on Big Mike's arm. Wouldn't the press love to know that Morgan Grady was really Morgan O'Connell from Roxbury, not Beacon Hill?

Charlotte had found out and look what had happened. She'd hadn't just left him. She'd run away.

Morgan couldn't do this anymore. Rose had said to throw the media a bone, to give them a story. A story…

Morgan Grady gets married.

Morgan Grady no longer a bachelor.

No longer sexy, now just a boring old married man…a very boring Morgan Grady.

Morgan took a deep breath and the pressure in his chest began to ease.

He'd get married, get away from the hype, get back to being just a regular guy.

And it came to him as the tension melted, that he knew the perfect woman, knew the most sensible, practical woman who handled the press with ease, could manage his schedule, and already knew his many foibles—Winnie.

She'd been the best damn secretary. She'd be the best damn wife.

In the end, Winnie went to the interview at Osborne Manufacturing. It didn't seem right to cancel at the last minute and she thought she'd be smart to keep some avenues open. But while Mr. Osborne was just as nice in person as he'd been on the phone, Winnie knew the life she wanted wasn't in Charleston. The life she wanted was on Wall Street in downtown Manhattan, and just thinking of Morgan made her heart jump, more pain than pleasure in the swift rush of emotion.

On the late flight from Charleston to New York, Winnie plucked the pins from her chignon, freeing her hair. It fell past her shoulders in a heavy tumble.

The plane touched down in one big bump. Drooping a little in her taupe suit, she filed out with the other passengers, hair still loose, her travel bag dangling from her shoulder.

She'd kill for a long soak in the tub, followed by a pint of Rocky Road ice cream. No, make that a half gallon. To hell with her diet. Diets didn't work anyway. All the experts said so.

Wearily, she moved with the crowd through the terminal until she reached the curb, searching past the whizzing cars and buses for an available taxi.

"Need a lift?"

Him, it was him. Winnie half closed her eyes, thinking she'd never grow tired of that voice, never grow tired of the rich husky inflection. Air catching in her throat she turned around.

"Hello, Morg—Mr. Grady." It was the first time she'd slipped like that. Must have been the glass of wine she'd had on the plane on the way back.

He smiled faintly, creases fanning from his eyes, making him even sexier than ever. "Hello, Willa."

"Winnie."

"I know." His smile stretched and moving forward he took her travel bag from her and slung it on his own shoulder. "How did the interview go?"

"Fine." She frowned a little, realizing that he was here at the airport when he was supposed to be out to dinner with members of his board. "What are you doing here?"

"I came for you."

"Your shareholder's meeting—"

"Canceled." His mouth quirked but he wasn't exactly smiling anymore. In fact, he looked fierce, hard. "I was waiting at the gate but somehow missed you," he added, gesturing toward the terminal, black blazer falling open over his fine knit black shirt. He almost always wore black.

"Ah, there's my car now," he said. "We'll talk on the way."

She fell into step beside him. "Talk on the way where?"

"Dinner."

Nothing was making sense, she thought, reaching up to rub her temple, her thick hair falling forward against her cheek. She felt so tired and unkempt. Her hair down, her suit creased, her feet aching. And he wanted to take her to dinner now, like this?

She'd fantasized about having dinner with him but it hadn't been like this in her fantasy. In her fantasy she felt fresh, elegantly dressed, relaxed. In her fantasy she'd been in control.

That certainly wasn't the case now.

The limousine pulled next to the curb, black and sleek. Morgan opened the limo's back door. "Come," he encouraged. "I don't want to miss our dinner reservation. I've already pushed it back twice."

Winnie flashed him a worried glance before sliding into the back of the luxurious limousine. As the car pulled from the curb he pushed a dozen long-stemmed red roses into her arms, the stems perfectly straight, tied with a wide purple silk ribbon, and the roses still in identically shaped buds.

He'd never given her flowers before. Not even on Secretaries Day.

Winnie's heart twisted, a jagged little pain going through her middle. She was surprised how much all this hurt. She'd always wanted this from him but now that it was happening, it was wrong. It felt wrong.

Flowers were supposed to mean something, she thought wildly. Dinner was part of romance. But this wasn't romance. This was business.

He wanted her back. He was determined to get her back. She clutched the flowers so tightly they shook in her hands.

"He offered you the job?" Morgan's voice sliced through the dim interior, an edge to his voice, anger, too.

She jerked her head up. Her gaze met his. "Yes."

"Did you accept it?"

"Not yet," she answered, drawing a swift breath, drinking in the fragrance he wore. It was relatively light but on him it made her head swim.

She loved the way he smelled. He didn't always wear cologne, but when he did, it knocked her off balance, affected her coordination. Other men wore the same cologne but it didn't make her dizzy and hungry to bury her face against the neck and just breathe him in...

"Good. Because I have something to propose to you."

"What?"

"Let's wait until we get to the restaurant. I just ask you to keep an open mind."

An open mind? What did he mean by that?

Nervous, Winnie drew the flowers up and sniffed the blossoms. Compared to him, they had no fragrance, no spicy or musky scent, nothing like the roses in her mother's garden.

She glanced at him and his blue gaze locked with hers. The intensity in his expression took her breath away.

"An open mind," he repeated softly as the limousine pulled off the interstate and made a series of turns before drawing up in front of a small rustic restaurant with a nearly deserted parking lot. "That's all I ask."

The driver parked in front of the restaurant, put the car in neutral, and hurried around the side to open the door.

"Where are we?" she asked, sliding across the leather seat and stepping out into the warm night.

"We're just outside the city. This is Franco's. It's a favorite place of mine."

As Morgan stepped aside to let her pass, a car pulled out of the shadows, headlights blinding, and drew next to them. Morgan muttered an oath and Winnie glanced at him in alarm. The driver of the car leaned out and a camera flash exploded in their eyes. Morgan's driver charged the photographer.

"Come on, let's get inside," Morgan urged her, shielding her eyes from the blinding strobe of light.

She wanted to move, but fear and too much adrenaline held her in place.

It wasn't until the photographer peeled out of the

parking lot, tires screaming as the car rounded the corner that she let go of Morgan.

She drew a shuddering breath, trying to calm herself. She'd been so afraid. When the photographer had first pulled up, she'd thought it was a gun he held, not a camera, and she'd felt absolute terror when the flash exploded.

All her fears about big city life and crime had come to life. She felt violated. Her safety stripped.

Trembling, she turned on Morgan. "What was that about?"

He shook his head, shadows in his eyes. "Just more of the same."

She drew another shuddering breath. "That was awful."

"I'm sorry."

"He had no right."

"They do it all the time, Winnie."

Morgan's voice was quietly apologetic, but she heard his frustration. He endured this on a daily basis lately.

She was beginning to calm down but she still felt chilled, and her nerves were jittery. "It's just such a shock. Where did he come from? How did he know you were here?"

"He probably followed the limo from the airport."

"You mean he's been tailing you this whole time?"

He sighed wearily. "Most likely."

Winnie was horrified. She glanced out, to the street and beyond. "They need to leave you alone."

"They will. Eventually." He reached toward her, placed a light hand on her back. "You're all right now?"

Her anger had dissipated, and the shock was wearing off, but she wasn't all right. She felt hot and tingly, and just the light pressure of his hand made her feel too sensitive.

He'd never touched her in six months of working for him and his hand sent rippling shock waves through her middle. "I'm fine," she answered, her voice huskier than normal.

The restaurant door opened and a gentleman in a red smoking jacket and black trousers stood in the doorway. "Mr. Grady, we've been expecting you. Welcome."

"Hello, Franco. Thanks for accommodating us."

Morgan steered her up the three front steps. She felt his warmth and it was a tangible thing.

Franco led them to a table at the back. The restaurant was dark and dimly lit, with deep crimson cloths and lots of little votive candles on what would otherwise be empty tables.

Winnie slid out of her blazer and Franco took it with him. Winnie felt a little naked in the cream silk blouse but tried to focus on other things. "Is Franco's Italian or French?" What a dumb question. "I guess it doesn't matter," she added quickly. "It could be either. Italian or French."

She was babbling. She was barely coherent. This evening was going to be bad.

"Don't be so nervous. This is just me. Morgan Grady. That jerk of a boss you work for—"

"Don't," she wailed, slinking lower in her seat. "Please don't bring that up now."

He smiled. "I'm playing."

He played? That was a revelation. "Okay."

Morgan had been studying her. "Now I know why I missed you at the gate," he said, almost relieved. "You don't look like you. I was looking for the—" he pointed to his head, finger circling "—braids."

"Oh."

He was still staring at her. "I've never seen you wear your hair down."

"Not by choice, no. But I had a headache earlier, on the plane, so I took the bobby pins out." He didn't say anything and she shifted uncomfortably. "You don't like my hair down, do you? It is on the messy side—"

"It's nice. I'm just not used to seeing you like this, but it—you—look very nice."

His voice had deepened and she felt absolutely terrified again. This wasn't normal. She didn't know what to do, or what to say. It didn't help when Franco arrived with a bottle of champagne.

Champagne. Her heart did a painful flip. Morgan was really going all out.

Franco held the bottle before Morgan, waiting for his approval, and once getting it, pushed the cork off with a soft pop.

Her first bottle of real champagne, French champagne, in a restaurant named Franco's with *News Weekly*'s Man of the Year. This wasn't her life. She was living Morgan's ex-girlfriend Annika's life. Only problem was, she didn't know how to be Annika.

Winnie smiled nervously as Morgan filled her glass before filling his. The champagne was a pale gold and very fizzy. Hundreds of tiny bubbles rose swiftly to the surface and she realized she'd better say something intelligent soon, do something semi-sophisticated.

Winnie seized her flute. "To *News Weekly*'s Man of the Year," she proposed, voice quavering. "Congratulations, Morgan. You deserve it."

She sounded so sincere, so artless, Morgan thought, lifting his glass and clinking his flute against hers. The candlelight flattered her, her pale skin luminous in the candle's flickering yellow-white light.

She wasn't like the women he dated. She was far more grounded, more real. He liked her lack of sophistication; it suited him better than glamour and glitz. Everyone assumed because he'd made enormous sums of money that he liked the trappings, preferred the trappings. The opposite was true.

"It's been quite a year," she added. "You're everyone's favorite person."

"Not yours," he answered mockingly.

Her cheeks turned pink. Her gaze dropped to the tablecloth. "You're talking about the book, but I really do hate it when you bring this up because the last six months have been amazing. I mean, let's face it. You're amazing."

Something in her voice wrapped around his heart. She had a softness in her that constantly surprised him. He didn't know many women anymore that were still so tender, still so…innocent.

Morgan frowned, momentarily confused. He wasn't entirely comfortable with this slight shift in feeling. He wasn't comfortable with feeling, period, but he hadn't selected her as a wife candidate based on emotion. It was reason. She was the most logical choice.

"And to think a week ago I felt underappreciated," she said with a wry smile. "I guess I can't feel that way now, can I?"

"You felt underappreciated?"

"You didn't even know my name!"

He felt a stab of guilt. That was bad. She had a right to be upset, but she also had to learn to accept responsibility for herself. Stand on her own two feet. "I wish you'd corrected me the first time I said it wrong. Tapped me on the shoulder, buzzed me on the intercom—"

"Would never happen," she interrupted with another husky laugh, and in the candlelight he realized her eyes were a hazel green, mostly green, with just a touch of yellow. "You…you're…you."

"Brilliant deduction, Miss Graham."

She smiled at him, pink suffusing her cheeks and something shifted inside him yet again. This emotion was new, and rather protective, and more than a little bit jealous.

Mr. Osborne couldn't have her. Morgan wasn't going to lose her.

Dinner over, Franco cleared their plates and the empty champagne bottle was replaced with coffee. Winnie leaned back against the booth, relaxed, sated.

"Lovely," she sighed and then was forced to cover her mouth to smother a yawn. She hadn't looked at her watch but it had to be way past midnight. "This was like a dream."

"It doesn't have to end." Morgan leaned forward, black knit shirt pushed up on his muscular forearms. "I have an idea, and it's going to sound a little crazy, but I think it'd work, and I think we'd both be happy."

"You're going to give me a raise?"

His eyes met hers and held. They were such a dark blue, gleaming like water beneath a full moon. "You could say that."

He reached down, drew a small black-velvet jeweler's box from his trouser pocket and set it on the table.

Winnie's heart stopped for a moment. She felt odd, a prickly sensation shooting from her middle to her limbs.

He slid the jeweler's box across the table. "Marry me."

She'd begun to shake. She felt so cold. She couldn't believe he'd do this. She couldn't believe he'd treat her this way. "That's not funny." Her hands felt stiff as she groped about on the seat for her purse before remembering she'd left it in the limo.

"I'm not making a joke."

"Put it away," she choked.

"Winnie—"

"Don't Winnie me." She felt naked in her silk blouse, bereft with her hair down. It was as if he'd caught her skinny-dipping. She felt so bare, so exposed.

Winnie slipped out of the booth and onto her feet. "Don't get up," she said quickly, cheeks feverish, her skin burning with shame. And she did feel shame. She felt completely humiliated. "I'll just grab a cab."

Morgan dropped cash on the table and followed quickly. "Wait, Winnie." He barred her exit with an arm strategically placed across the doorway. "Don't leave. Not like this."

"I think we've both had enough drama for one evening," she choked, unable to look at him, her arms bundled across her chest.

He'd always thought of her as comfortable and solid, but without her blazer he realized she wasn't very big at all and definitely not comfortable and solid. He could see the outline of a delicate collarbone through her thin silk blouse and the slender bra strap across her straight back. With her head averted he glimpsed her neck and the pale creamy skin beneath her ear. She looked so small. And terribly defenseless.

"Winnie, don't be angry. I'm not trying to hurt you. I'm trying to tell you that I need you."

Need her? Winnie thought, trying hard to keep the tears from falling. He didn't need her. He was Morgan Grady, New York's Sexiest Bachelor. How could he need anything? "This is like a prank high school boys play. This is something they'd do—set you up, make you feel special, and then humiliate you afterward. But I never, ever would have expected this from *you*."

He caught her by the shoulders. "But this isn't a joke. The proposal is real, and I'm very sincere, but obviously I approached it wrong."

She closed her eyes. "Have some pity, please."

But he wouldn't stop talking and his fingers dug into her shoulders. "I should have told you at the outset that this is business. I should have prefaced the proposal by telling you it's a job. I do want to marry you but it wouldn't be all fun and games. There's the media to contend with, and tremendous social pressure, but I'd take care of you financially. I'd make sure you had everything your heart desires."

His fingers tightened yet again. "Everything," he repeated more forcefully.

The Wedding Of The Year! New York papers proclaimed. Wall Street's Most Eligible Bachelor No Longer Available.

Winnie tried to avoid reading the papers, not wanting to get caught up in the hype but every now and then she'd sit back at her desk and stare off into space and just smile. She, Winnie Graham, was marrying Morgan Grady in just four weeks.

There was paperwork to sign, a contract and a rather tersely worded prenuptial agreement, but the business aspect didn't bother her. He needed her, and that was enough.

Planning the wedding was even more exciting. For the first time in years she and her mother had something in common and they spent hours on the phone discussing wedding traditions and making decisions about the ceremony and reception.

Winnie confided to her mother one evening that she felt like Cinderella getting ready for the ball. Everything was just so perfect, Winnie enthused, life couldn't be better.

"You really love him, don't you?" her mother had said gently, maternal pride in her voice. It was almost as if she couldn't believe that Winnie, her most awkward daughter, would soon be a radiant bride.

"Of course!" Winnie didn't even have to think about it. There were no questions in her mind. She was doing the right thing. Morgan needed her and she needed him. "I'm crazy about him. I couldn't love anyone more."

Her mother hesitated. "And you're sure he's right for you?"

"Mother, I *love* Morgan."

Her mother hesitated even longer this time. "Yes, darling, but are you sure he loves you?"

CHAPTER SIX

MORGAN glanced at his watch. That must be a record. It'd taken five frantic weeks to put the wedding together and only twenty-three minutes to empty the congested church, call the St. Regis, and cancel the reception.

Thank God everyone had gone, and having given the priest a generous contribution to the church, Morgan headed to his waiting limousine, unfastening his snug bow tie as he walked.

Who said lightning didn't strike twice? Twice he'd been engaged, twice he'd planned a wedding and both times the bride bolted.

What the hell was wrong with him?

He'd proposed to Charlotte out of love, and proposed to Winnie out of need, but both brides had turned around and run.

So much for Sexiest Man in New York.

Swearing, Morgan slid off his coat. All he wanted now was a cold drink, a change of clothes, and his plane. He was getting out of this miserable city for the rest of the summer and figure out just what had gone wrong with his life from the very private, very pristine island he owned in the Bahamas.

But on reaching his limousine he discovered Winnie's parents waiting for him. Mrs. Graham was crying. Mr. Graham looked stoic. And Morgan really didn't want to talk to either of them.

"Do you have a minute, Morgan?" Mr. Graham asked, still dressed in his black tux, sweat beading his brow. It was damn hot, unbearably hot with not a hint of breeze anywhere.

Morgan paused. He didn't feel like talking. He had no desire to make any conversation but he couldn't very well brush off Winnie's parents. He might be furious with Winnie but he didn't hate her.

"Of course," Morgan answered, wondering for the first time if perhaps the prenuptial agreement he'd presented to her had been too terse. It'd been business to him but really, had he been fair with her? Could he have been more generous financially?

Mr. Graham cleared his throat. "We're not happy at all about what happened today. Winnie's mother and I want you to know—"

"She was wrong," Winnie's mother interrupted tearfully. "There's no excuse. I don't know what came over her. She's always been a little high-strung, but really to run off like that..." Mrs. Graham shook her head, peach-lipstick lips quivering. "It makes no sense at all, especially as she's so crazy about you."

At least Winnie had done something right, he thought grimly, trying to keep his expression pleasant as he ground his teeth together. She'd convinced her parents she was marrying for love, something that all parents wanted to believe. Including his.

"I guess she had second thoughts," he said, jaw aching with the effort it took to maintain a smile.

"For whatever it's worth, she does love you. She's absolutely head over heels in love with you. And if you don't believe me, ask her yourself—"

"Margie," Mr. Graham remonstrated, placing a hand on his wife's arm. "Don't do that to Winnie."

"But it's true," Mrs. Graham vigorously defended. "Winnie can't lie. Her face gives her away. She gets a tic, on the left side. We use to catch her all the time when she was small."

A tic? On the left side? Morgan rolled his eyes as he stepped from the elevator in his building to his third-floor apartment. Give me a break, he thought, opening his door and stepping in. He didn't need that kind of nonsense today.

Mr. Foley appeared from the cool air-conditioned recesses of Morgan's apartment. "Would you care for a drink, sir?" he asked, taking Morgan's tuxedo jacket and cast-off tie.

"A cola on ice would be great."

"I'm sorry about today, sir—"

"I don't want to talk about it."

"Of course." Mr. Foley inclined his head but he didn't budge.

Morgan suppressed a sigh. "Yes, Mr. Foley?"

"Is she all right, sir?"

Morgan wished he could pretend he didn't know what Mr. Foley was talking about. He wished he were already in his plane on his way to St. Jermaine's, his tiny island with the most beautiful white sand anywhere in the world. But he wasn't on his plane, and he'd just come from the cathedral and he couldn't forget that Winnie had a tic when she lied and that somehow her mother earnestly believed that Winnie loved him.

Winnie, his dutiful talented assistant, loved him.

What were the words Marge Graham had used? *Head over heels.*

"I'm sure she's all right," Morgan answered wearily, feeling the first pang of guilt. But he didn't want to feel guilty, there was no reason to feel guilty, it wasn't as if he was taking advantage of her. She was being compensated. Cash, savings account, new penthouse, credit cards in her name...

And she'd left it all, and him. She'd run off, jumping into a yellow taxicab, her white skirts filling up the car's back seat.

Morgan had chased after her to the steps of the cathedral, had watched the taxi pull away from the curb into the stream of traffic. He'd gotten a glimpse of Winnie from the back window, saw a sheen of white, and pale skin. Saw her hand reach up and press tiara and veil to the top of her head.

Did she love him?

He told himself it didn't matter, that a contract was a contract, and business was business, but it did nothing to assuage his growing guilt.

If she loved him, it changed everything. He hadn't been strategic at all. Instead he'd taken advantage of a naive young woman's affection.

Winnie dragged her crescent-shaped tiara and starchy white veil from the top of her head, plucked the pins that twisted curls back from her face and slumped at her desk, chin in hand.

Well, the fairy tale was finally over.

The prince had kissed the frog who claimed to be a

princess and it turned out the frog was really just a frog and very green and very lumpy.

Winnie had never felt like such a lumpy green frog in all her life. There was no more pretending, no more fantasies of true love. She'd taken those three little words, *I need you,* and turned them into something huge and elaborate—a castle in the air.

Yes, he needed her, but not the way she wanted him to need her. He just needed a smokescreen. A shield. A semiwarm body to deter the press.

She'd been fine with that, too, had told herself that being needed was practically the same thing as being loved, but standing in the church, dressed up like a princess bride, she realized she might be able to delude the press, but she couldn't delude herself. She was too much of a romantic to settle for marriage without love.

Sighing at her folly, and wondering if she'd just messed up her one chance to do something really different with her life, Winnie rolled back in her chair, away from her desk, to look around the office.

This was Morgan's world. She'd loved his world.

She'd really miss his world.

For a moment she couldn't move, could hardly breathe, remembering how she'd come here four years ago on a job interview.

She was fresh out of college and Grady Investments was looking to hire an entry-level position for their research department. Grady Investments was Wall Street's hottest investment firm and they only took on the best and the brightest for their research team and Winnie had been thrilled when they read her résumé and requested an interview.

She spent two weeks preparing for the interview. She read every Fortune 500 press release available, tracked the hot stocks and graphed companies she believed were overvalued.

Winnie couldn't have been more prepared. Yet when she arrived for the interview she bombed. It was just like at the church today. She started thinking and criticizing herself and before she knew it she lost all her confidence.

She stood in Grady Investments's entry, hugging her briefcase that still had the new leather smell and she watched the people come and go through the reception area, all deep in conversation or engrossed in reading, and she felt like a fish out of water.

She wasn't smart like these people. She wasn't sophisticated like these people. She wasn't successful like these people.

The longer she stood there the more nervous she became. By the time she was led to the conference room for her appointment, she was a mess. Every intelligent thought had left her brain. Less than five minutes into the interview, Winnie apologized, picked up her portfolio, and ran.

It wasn't until she reached the busy street that the terror gave way to grief. Despite her degree, her university honors, and the expensive wool suit, she still couldn't do anything right.

That botched interview changed her career path. Instead of pursuing entry-level positions in finance she accepted a clerical position with another finance company. Her future had been decided.

Just like it'd been decided today.

Morgan had given her the opportunity of a lifetime—so what if he didn't love her? She could still have been part of his world and traveled and tried new things—but no, she had to overanalyze and overthink and ruin everything.

She'd blown it again.

"Going somewhere, Winnie?"

That voice was the voice she'd heard on the intercom for the last seven months and she responded to it even now, heart accelerating. *Morgan.* Slowly, Winnie turned in her chair, hands resting on her white silk skirt. "What are you doing here?"

"Looking for you."

Her stomach did a somersault, her pulse leaped, and she felt like a teenager all over again. "I'm here."

"So I see," he said, advancing toward her and moving the box from her desk to the ground. He sat on the edge of the desk, facing her. "How are you?"

Her stomach flip-flopped again. He'd changed from his tuxedo, but even dressed down, casual in a black knit shirt and khaki slacks, he looked gorgeous. The black shirt made his eyes look bluer, his hair glossier, his jaw more pronounced.

"Fine." She swallowed convulsively, nerves and tears battling for each other. "How are you?"

"Fine."

The strained civility made her want to laugh. Or cry. This had been one of the worst days of her life. She had no idea what would happen now.

Morgan hesitated, appeared to pick his words with care. "It was rather awkward with you leaving so suddenly."

She had a mental picture of him standing up front at the altar with the priest and the ring boy and the flower girl watching Winnie turn around, white skirts billowing, as she ran.

It was an awful mental picture and she pressed her nails to her skirt to erase it. "Was it that terrible?"

One of his black eyebrows lifted. "What do you think?"

So it was really terrible. No use kidding herself. He'd been humiliated. Winnie swallowed hard around the lump filling her throat. "I'm sorry."

He shrugged. "Fortunately I've been through this before so I'm getting adept at handling high-strung brides."

Her eyebrows puckered. "Be serious."

"I am." He smiled faintly, but hard glints shone in his dark blue eyes. "Don't believe me? Ask my mother. Rose will tell you all about it. It was fifteen years ago. Her name was Charlotte and I thought we were deeply in love."

Winnie didn't know what to say. The office seemed too huge and empty, too silent. She flexed her fingers, knuckles aching. "Did she really leave you at the altar, too?"

A small muscle pulled in his jaw. "Not exactly. She gave me a little more notice—she was kind enough to cancel a week before. But that didn't make it less difficult. People want to know what happened. They don't want to ask, and most don't, but every now and then you get the daring few who do."

"What was her reason for canceling?"

His shoulders shifted and he walked to the window

to gaze out at the enormous Federal Reserve Bank of New York. "It's complicated, but the bottom line was that she had concerns about my..." He hesitated, searching for the correct words. "Family tree."

The Gradys were one of the oldest most-respected families in Boston. How could anyone have a problem with his family? "That doesn't make sense."

He looked at her over his shoulder, his expression almost mocking. "It does if you know my family tree. In terms of lineage, I'm an O'Connell, not a Grady. Charlotte didn't discover this until a couple weeks before our wedding and she panicked—" he broke off, wincing at the word "—changed her mind. She didn't want an O'Connell. She wanted a Grady. A *real* Grady."

Winnie struggled to assimilate his words, and the meaning. "You're not Rose and Reed Grady's son?"

"I'm their *adopted* son." His lips twisted tighter, his smile harder.

"Same thing."

"Not to Charlotte."

Indignant, Winnie rose from her chair. "Then she didn't deserve you! She doesn't have a heart and she never loved you—"

"Who are you to talk about love?" He interrupted, facing her. "You weren't marrying me for love, were you?"

Winnie turned away, she couldn't look at him, couldn't answer. She hated lying. Was terrible at lying. Her parents used to say she couldn't keep any wrong a secret.

"Do you love me?" he repeated, walking toward her, tension in every muscle of his body.

Winnie sat down again, still averting her head. But Morgan turned her chair toward him so she couldn't avoid his gaze.

She touched her tongue to her upper lip. "I—"

"You what?"

"I care about you. Yes, definitely, I care about you. I've worked with you for seven months now. We've worked closely together in the last month, too."

"But you don't love me. This was business, right?"

She slowly looked up at him, her eyes wide, her expression anxious. "Mmm-hmm."

"Say it. Tell me with words."

Winnie took a quick breath. "I don't love you," she blurted, but even as she said the words, her cheek tightened and her left eye twitched.

Morgan stood, backed away, forehead deeply furrowed. Winnie watched him cross the floor, rub his nape, ruffling his hair.

"Was it hard to get over her?" she asked softly, thinking of this beautiful but callous Charlotte.

He shrugged carelessly, broad shoulders twisting beneath the snug black knit fabric. "She was beautiful, elegant, graceful." His hard expression eased, turning rueful. "Yes. It was."

"I'm sorry she hurt you."

His smile faded. "It was a long time ago. I was just a kid." He took a step back, sat down again on the desk. "Fifteen years," he said softly. "Fifteen years and I'm facing the same problem. How ironic."

Yes, she thought, ironic was the word for it because

seeing Morgan now, being alone with Morgan now, made her realize she'd made a huge mistake today, running away from the church.

"So what do we do?" he asked.

"I don't know."

"We can't stay here forever."

"No."

"We're going to need food, rest, a change of clothes."

That's right. Clothes. Winnie glanced down at her lavish wedding gown with the snug off-the-shoulder sleeves and the tiny crystals stitched across the fitted bodice. She could see the headlines in the morning paper: Bride-to-be Jilts Grady At The Altar. Man of the Year Claims Runaway Fiancée At The Office. "Photographers outside?"

He grimaced. "In droves."

Of course. When weren't there? Morgan Grady was still everyone's favorite bachelor. "I didn't bring anything with me."

"I've got some clean dress shirts in the closet in my office. You could wear one of my button-down shirts out with a pair of gym shorts. It's not high fashion but it's better than petticoats and silk."

Winnie changed in his office but needed his help to undo the endless little hooks hidden on the back of the dress.

It was strange having him help undress her. They'd never been so personal before, never dealt with much beyond contracts and copies, flight plans and schedules. His hands against her back, his fingers against her bare skin made her feel so much, made her want new things.

His hands, his mouth, his body, him...

She was glad he couldn't see her face, glad he couldn't see her blushing. Winnie Graham, she silently lectured herself, you're not his type, you'll never be his type, and just because you've made a deal with him doesn't mean it'll ever be love.

Hooks unfastened, Morgan left her alone to finish undressing and Winnie slipped out of the white boned corset, unclasped the white garter belt and rolled down the white silk stockings.

She stepped into the gray cotton gym shorts he'd left on his desk and then slid her arms into his starched blue pin-striped shirt. The shirttail hung down to the middle of her thighs leaving just two inches of shorts peeking beneath.

Winnie buttoned the pin-striped shirt to her breast-bone and rolled up the long sleeves so they no longer extended past her hands.

There. No longer a bride. Just plain old Winnie in Morgan's blue-striped shirt.

They rode the elevator down together, and Winnie spotted the cluster of photographers outside.

"I can't do this," she whispered, panicked all over again. "I know what the papers are going to say and it'll be horrible."

"Pretend then everything's fine."

"I can't, Morgan. That's the problem, I can't fake anything important—"

"Relax," he said as he wrapped an arm around her and brought her close against him so that her cheek nestled against his chest. She could feel his warmth and smell his skin and she felt comforted. "Take a deep breath."

She did. She stood there, close against him, and just breathed him in. Oh, heaven. This was heaven.

His hand gently rubbed up and down her back. His voice was firm, soothing. "We'll go out, we'll smile, we'll act like everything's fine. You can do that."

Immediately she stiffened. "I don't know—"

"Sure you can. You're with me, and you trust me, right?"

She looked up into his eyes, those amazing dark blue eyes, and his gaze was steady, his expression warm. He made her believe she could do anything. "Right."

They exited the lobby through a side door, but the photographers rushed toward them as the limousine pulled up at the curb.

It was still hot outside, the air heavy and sticky, and the flash of camera strobes blinded Winnie. The chauffeur had opened the back door but Morgan paused for the cameras, slid his hand low on Winnie's back and smiled.

And then the panic struck. "This isn't going to work," she choked, turning her face away from the cameras, her mouth pressed close to his chest.

"You just have to stop thinking. Let it go. Have fun," he answered, his lips against the curve of her ear.

"How?"

"Like this," he said, his voice dropping lower, deeper as he tilted her face up to his.

He was going to kiss her.

He was going kiss her *here?* Panic flooded her, drowning all rational thought. She jerked as his head dropped, but he held her firmly, his palms flat against her middle, one at her back, one at her belly.

"Relax," he repeated, just before his mouth brushed hers. "It's just a kiss."

Just a kiss, she silently repeated and then gave in to the incredible sensation of his lips slowly, very slowly covering hers.

His mouth felt cool against her hot skin, his lips were firm and he drew her closer, bringing her snugly against the hard plane of his chest and the roughness of his jaw and chin. He was built so much bigger, and harder and it crossed her mind that he knew everything about making love and she knew absolutely nothing.

But expertise seemed inconsequential as his mouth moved leisurely across hers. He was doing something to her, making a deep dormant part of her come to life. The touch of his mouth against hers was about as wonderful sensation as she could imagine, and as his breath fanned her skin, she shuddered, her body rippling in a series of explosions, nerve endings bursting into flames.

Winnie forgot everything but touch, and the newness of his touch, sighing with pleasure as the pressure of his lips increased. She welcomed the heat and the flick of his tongue against the inside of her lower lip.

Her mouth felt warm, she felt warm, she felt wildly alive. Heat coiled in her middle, heat and urgency and something so physical she craved more of him but didn't know what. Tentatively she touched his chest, fingers splaying against the thick band of muscle.

"See?" he said, his head lifting just enough to gaze into her eyes. "Kissing's easy."

The photographers got their shot, she thought

numbly, as the limousine sailed through Manhattan traffic. He might hate the media attention, might dread the photographers, but he always managed a smile and a civil word.

He was amazing that way, she thought, glancing at him in the deepening twilight. Back there, at the Tower's building, one of the reporters had asked Morgan how it'd felt, being left at the altar, and Morgan had grinned, flashing white teeth.

"Felt a little awkward," he answered with the easy confidence that charmed even tabloid journalists. "But I have her now, and that's all that matters."

She turned to look out the tinted window at the flicker of light and shadow, the moon beginning to peek between skyscrapers and glimpses of water. No wonder people loved Morgan. He was everything the public admired—intelligent, articulate, insightful—and he broke hearts.

"You do that so well," Winnie said. "You're a PR dream."

"I don't feel like it."

"Then you fake it well."

"Learned early."

She felt cold on the inside, empty on the inside. She'd loved the kiss but it'd just been good PR for him. Everything about them was just appearances. "How did you learn to fake it?"

He shrugged. "Rather Darwinian. Survival of the fittest, I suppose. People don't want to know about problems and troubles. They want success stories. I try to give them a success story."

"So you do what you have to do?"

"That's right."

Her emotions felt dangerously unhinged. "Including kissing me."

He turned, stared at her, his gaze unflinching. "It wasn't exactly a chore."

She took a moment to answer, wondering why her heart was beating so fiercely and why she had this odd weak sensation in her tummy. "I know you're not attracted to me. You prefer models. Tall blond supermodels, preferably from Sweden."

"I liked kissing you."

"No, you didn't."

"And I'd like to kiss you again but I think we have a few things to straighten out first. Our relationship, for example."

Winnie was growing increasingly uncomfortable. "We don't have a relationship—"

"We do. We had one at the office and we came awfully close to getting married today so obviously there's something here, even if it's just friendship, and that alone deserves discussion."

"It's going to be hard to discuss anything right now. Emotions are running awfully high."

"Which is why we need some time. I think it'd be wise if we both went away for a few weeks, put some distance between us and the gossip columnists and figure out what we're going to do next."

Truthfully, she'd love to get away for a few weeks. She felt trapped right now, trapped and claustrophobic.

Winnie chewed on her lower lip. "Where are you thinking of going?"

"St. Jermaine's."

His island off the Berry Islands in the Bahamas. She thought longingly of turquoise water and sandy coves and the shade provided by coconut trees.

"I guess I could go home," she said slowly, trying to figure out her best escape plan. "Mom and Dad will be upset but I can't imagine them kicking me out."

Morgan muttered an exasperated oath. "I'm not leaving you here to face the media alone. The pressure will be intense. If I head to St. Jermaine's, I'm taking you with me."

CHAPTER SEVEN

THEY weren't flying out until the morning and Morgan spent much of the night sitting in a leather chair in his living room staring out at Manhattan's sparkling skyline.

She did love him.

Damn. This wasn't supposed to happen. He didn't want her emotionally involved. He knew what it felt like to love someone and not be loved in return. It hurt. It was miserable. He wouldn't wish that kind of feeling on his worst enemy and Winnie was definitely not his enemy.

Hell, he liked her. A lot. And she'd looked pretty today, almost glamorous, although part of him preferred her without the eye makeup and hair goop. Winnie didn't need cosmetics to cover her up or try to improve her. She was great just the way she was.

Everything was great until today.

What had happened at the church? What scared her?

Sighing, Morgan rubbed his jaw, the bristles of his beard scraping his palm. She loved him. Fine. He liked her.

In fact, he'd really liked kissing her. She had a great mouth, incredibly lush lips, and sex would be just as pleasurable once they got past the early, awkward stage.

The early, awkward stage.

That's it, he thought, sitting up. That's where he went wrong.

He'd been rushing her too much, pressuring her without meaning to. She needed time to grow comfortable with him, with them.

He knew without asking that she wasn't sexually experienced. There was an innocent air about her. Even the way she looked at him was youthful, hopeful, lacking pretension. He knew she rarely dated. In fact, he didn't know when she'd last gone out.

No wonder she was scared. She probably stood there at the back of the church listening to the heavy-handed organist, overpowered by the lilies, and imagined all the things she'd never done, wondering if sex with him would even be enjoyable or if it'd be something she'd have to endure like the Victorian wife who stared at the ceiling, gritting her teeth and bearing it for God and country.

He reluctantly smiled. Poor Winnie.

She had no idea that he'd never, ever rush her into bed. She hadn't a clue that he loved foreplay, loved the feel of a woman, and the unique way a woman was made. He relished curves, adored the female shape, and had a particular weakness for a soft, bare mouth.

Like Winnie's soft, bare mouth.

His body hardened just thinking about the kiss earlier. She'd shivered in his arms. He'd felt her helpless response and he knew then that if she responded to his kiss like that, she'd be just as sensitive in bed.

What he needed to do was woo her. Wine her, dine her, make impossibly slow love to her. She'd eventually discover that love wasn't the only thing that helped cement a relationship. He might not love her in the romantic poetry sense, but he could offer Winnie trust, respect, companionship, and best of all, sexual compatibility.

Morgan stood up, stretched, and gratefully headed for bed. Now that he'd identified the problem, he'd come up with a solution. Now, if he were lucky, he might even get a little sleep.

Morgan's bungalow on St. Jermaine's, if five thousand elegant square feet could be called a bungalow, looked like something out of *Architectural Digest.*

It was an absolutely stunning space, all creams and taupe, floor-to-ceiling windows that opened completely to let in the cool sea breeze, with gleaming hardwood floors.

Hands on her hips, Winnie inspected his collection of folk and Caribbean art. The bright canvases and sculpture were a contrast to the cool neutral walls and furniture.

"This is not a beach house," she said, transfixed by the canvases depicting trees and oceans, exploding volcanoes and dancing people.

"Sure it is. It's just got style, that's all," Morgan retorted as Mr. Foley moved past them, heading toward the kitchen where he intended to take control of the menu, the grocery list, and the cook.

During the three-hour flight from New York, Winnie had learned that Mr. Foley accompanied Morgan on most trips, ensuring Morgan's comfort and saving him from having to attend to irritating domestic details.

Rather like her job.

Although in her job she rarely left the office, and when she did, it was to sit across from Morgan in the limousine, take dictation, prep him for meetings, and make last-minute travel arrangements.

But she'd never been on his plane, or taken a trip anywhere with him until now.

When the Learjet landed an hour ago on St. Jermaine's narrow airstrip, Winnie felt a wave of excitement. For the next week she'd be virtually alone on a private tropical island with Morgan Grady, New York's Sexiest Bachelor. If that wasn't an adventure, she didn't know what was.

A young man in a bright print shirt driving a white Jeep had met them at the airstrip and ferried them the half mile to the house.

They'd driven through a dense grove of coconut trees on the way to the house and Winnie had peeled off her linen blazer to relish the island breeze. The blazer matched her beige linen skirt and without the blazer she was quite comfortable in her camisole top.

In the shade of the coconut grove Winnie drew a deep breath, feeling for the first time a moment of peace. With the emerald hills, turquoise cove, and white powdery sand, it almost felt like paradise.

Morgan took her on a brief tour of the house, showing her the central living areas before leading her down a wide, highly polished hallway to a very private wing of guestrooms.

"Your room's here," he said, opening a door, revealing a spacious suite decorated in apricot and cream. "I'm on the other side. There is a house phone, though, in case you need me."

She turned her back on the massive four-poster bed not wanting that kind of visual just now. "I won't need you."

One black eyebrow rose. "You sound so sure."

Winnie shrugged, feeling a little cavalier. She rather liked being with Morgan one on one, away from the office. She felt more equal, less dependent. It wasn't as if she needed his approval anymore. What was the worst that could happen now? He'd fire her?

"I won't need you," she said sweetly, crossing her arms over her chest. "If I think about the history of our *relationship,* it's *you* that needs *me.*"

His eyebrow arched higher. "How is it that I need you?"

She felt rather feisty just then, and more than a bit wicked. He'd always been so in control and she'd followed him around like a puppy dog.

Winnie smiled.

"You're the one always desperate to find me. At work you lean on the intercom, shoot constant e-mails to me, hound me by cell phone. In fact the last time I left my pager on my desk, you practically had a nervous breakdown."

"That's a gross exaggeration!"

Winnie took a step back as he stepped forward. "Maybe, but it's still true. When have I needed you for anything?"

Her arch question was met by complete silence. His dark blue eyes met hers, held, and she saw a flicker there, in the dark blue depths, a hot blue fire she'd never seen before.

Winnie felt a tiny thrill, followed by a surge of adrenaline. Morgan was looking at her, really looking at her, and he liked what he saw. It wasn't an external thing, it was something else, something deeper, more basic, and there was heat in his eyes, heat in the way he leaned a little closer and then a little closer.

Very slowly, very deliberately Morgan placed his right hand on the wall next to her shoulders, and then his left hand, trapping her there between him and the wall.

He leaned even closer, until their bodies were nearly touching.

"I think you have needs, Winnie."

His voice was so husky. His warmth was tangible. She felt her tummy tighten. "Of course I do. I need eight hours' sleep each night, three nutritious meals every day, twenty minutes' exercise—"

"Naked, in my bed."

Winnie's mouth dropped open, then blushing furiously, she snapped it closed. She scrambled to think of something to say but nothing smart or succinct came to mind.

Morgan leaned closer still, and whispered in her ear. "Actually, twenty minutes is nothing. I recommend a minimum of forty." Glints shone in his eyes. "Sixty whenever possible."

Still blushing, she lifted her chin, her heart beating faster in a one-two dance that made her feel very aware and very alive. "Thank you for the offer, *Mr.* Grady, but I believe there'll be plenty of exercise opportunities on St. Jermaine's without having to put yourself out."

"Really?"

She fought the urge to smile. Her imagination was

running wild just now. She could picture his style of warm-up, the vigorous aerobic activity and the recommended cool-down. "Better yet, the things I have in mind require *no* nudity."

"Nudity's nice."

"I prefer my clothes."

Morgan's mouth practically grazed her sensitive earlobe. "Then you haven't found the right...activity... yet."

She loved the feel of his lips on the curve of her ear and the tender skin below. A delicious shiver raced through her as he caught her ear between his teeth and held it there.

He was teasing her, tormenting her and she loved it. How bad was that? She actually liked that he was making her ache inside, making her feel a fierce and driving need.

"Come on, Winnie, admit that you'd enjoy nude activity with me."

She grinned. He made sex sound lighthearted, even fun. She was amused and intrigued. "I don't know. Maybe...after I'm tired of everything else there is to do on the island."

His lips touched her neck very briefly, very lightly. "Like what?"

"Everything," she sighed, voice dropping, heat growing.

"Name a few."

He kissed her just above her collarbone. It was a fleeting kiss but he seemed to know every nerve ending already. Winnie gasped softly as his tongue flicked the curve of collarbone.

"I'm waiting," he added, just before his mouth slid up her neck, back to her ear and she felt as if he'd set her skin on fire.

Winnie grabbed his shirt, practically clinging to his chest, and dragged herself closer, needing contact, much more contact.

"Swimming," she whispered, mouth drying, belly knotting. Oh, she wanted him to touch her, wanted his hands against her ribs, under her breasts, sliding down the length of her.

But he was too intent on keeping score. "That's one."

"Is that enough?"

"No," he answered, hands moving to cup her face and tilt her head, exposing her neck. His fingers caressed her nape. His lips kissed an invisible spot on her neck, a spot that seemed wired just for him because every time he touched her there she gripped his shirt tighter, pressed herself closer.

"You said endless," he reminded, tipping her head back so that his lips could travel up her neck to the width of her jaw.

He was touching her skin and tasting her skin and she'd never felt so much sensation in all her life. "Jogging," she choked.

"That's two."

"Jogging—"

"You already said that."

She felt his smile against her skin, felt the heat building between them. It was wild, it was something so new and yet so strong that she wriggled helplessly, seeking more contact, more pressure, more fulfillment. "Snorkeling, sailing, snorkeling, sailing...."

"Yes. But you can only count each one once."

"How about kissing?" she sighed, turning her head toward his, wanting his mouth, needing his lips.

He wouldn't kiss her though. He lifted his head and appeared to consider her question.

Winnie groaned. "Kiss me, Morgan, please."

He bent his elbows, leaned all the way in so that his chest crushed her breasts and his hips ground against hers and she felt the hard ridge of his erection against her thighs. But still he didn't kiss her, and suddenly she couldn't stand it a moment longer.

Groaning, Winnie reached up, clasped his neck and dragged his head down to hers. His mouth felt cool, he felt hard and strong and her lips parted beneath the pressure of his.

She wanted to open that way for him. Wanted to part her knees and let him in and feel him tight and hard against her skin.

Just wanting to know him, wanting to experience him, made her blood race, her body warming from the inside out. As his kiss deepened and his tongue thrust inside her mouth she felt herself soften, growing pliant against him. It was the most wonderful sensual awakening, a hint of what could be, a glimpse of what surrender would feel like.

The door banged open and the young man in the bright yellow print shirt burst in carrying Winnie's suitcase.

"Oh! Sorry," he apologized, quickly backing up once he'd realized he'd intruded.

But by then Winnie had jumped out from under Morgan's arm and Morgan was smiling faintly as he watched her smooth her linen skirt and top.

Her lips felt tender. Her body throbbed. She felt self-conscious once again.

"Thanks for the tour," she said briskly, trying to cover her embarrassment. "I think I now know where everything is."

His eyes met hers and his smile slowly stretched, laughter just beneath the surface, warmth in the blue depths. "Yes, I think I do, too."

He led her back to the center of the house, which had a distinct pavilion feel with the floor-to-ceiling windows and the oversize ceiling fans strategically positioned over dining and sitting areas.

Mr. Foley appeared as they returned to the living room. "A cold drink?" he asked, extending a sleek pewter tray.

"Thank you," Winnie said, accepting one of the tall glasses festively garnished with pineapple, banana and orange slices.

This was the life. She knew she was being spoiled, knew she'd never experience anything like this again. A small voice inside her urged her to savor every decadent cocktail, every breathtaking vista, every mind-blowing kiss, because before she knew it she'd be back in steamy New York, sweating on the subway's vinyl seat and wishing to high heaven that women's nylons had never been invented.

Morgan took his drink and Mr. Foley slid the tray beneath his arm. "There are hot and cold appetizers waiting,'' he said, gesturing toward the sunken living room.

"He's very formal,'' Winnie said as Mr. Foley marched down the hall back toward the kitchen.

"He's great, isn't he?'' Morgan answered, carrying his drink down the steps into the living room eclectically furnished with antiques and low comfortable pieces.

Winnie had yet to take a sip from her glass but she loved just looking at the luscious fresh fruit garnish. She hadn't had really ripe pineapple in ages.

She followed Morgan slowly, reminding herself to remember this moment, making note of the gentle breeze created by the ceiling fan and the blue sky outside now lit with horizontal streaks of pink and orange. Even the sky here looked ripe, edible, sensual.

Morgan watched her come down the steps and approach the rattan coffee table. She was beautiful, and her beauty was natural, the kind that glows from the inside, the kind that has nothing to do with hair and makeup and elegant clothes.

It was her lovely green-flecked eyes. Her soft sensitive mouth. Her light brown hair pulled back in a simple ponytail. He loved the lines of her neck. The shape of her lips. Her curves. Oh, those curves.

He'd felt her warmth earlier, felt the promise of her softness and he'd wanted her so bad that it was all he could do to keep it slow, take it easy, stay relaxed.

She was smiling now, smiling at some secret thought and he loved the way she bit her lower lip trying to keep her smile to herself.

"Do you like the drink?" Morgan asked, indicating the glass with the frothy white mixture.

"I haven't tried it yet. Let me find out." She lifted her glass, took a little sip. "It's a banana milkshake!" She laughed in surprise.

That smile just about did him in. His gut knotted, his body hardened. He wanted to drop her on the couch, slide his hands beneath her narrow linen skirt and— He shook his head, he wouldn't last the night if he didn't get some control.

"An adult banana milkshake," he corrected, "it's potent. Mr. Foley makes one very dangerous banana daiquiri."

She took another drink, this time a bigger swallow. "I don't taste any alcohol."

"Annika said the same thing—" Morgan broke off, mentally kicking himself. That was stupid.

Winnie had heard him. It was amazing the impact his words had on her. A moment ago she'd been so happy she literally glowed, and yet suddenly she crumpled. Folded in like a paper airplane

"Annika's been here?"

Of course she had. Annika had been his girlfriend for months but none of that mattered now. Annika was the past. Winnie was the present. Women should know these things but they never focused on the important facts.

Morgan stifled a sigh. "She came with me last spring, when we were dating."

"Did she like it here?"

"Winnie, don't do this."

But Winnie's chin was set, her expression fixed. "Did she come here often?"

"That's irrelevant. The important thing is you're here with me now."

Her eyes watered. "Yes, but that's just this week. It'll be someone else next week."

Morgan set his glass on the rattan coffee table. "I'm not going to even dignify that with a response."

She moved toward him, blocking his path. "Why not?"

"Because you're being ridiculous. You're acting…jealous, and you have no right to be jealous."

"Why not?"

"Because I proposed to you. I was at the church yesterday. I was standing with the priest at the altar in front of a huge crowd of people waiting for you. And guess what? You walked out on *me*."

Winnie didn't speak and he drew in a deep breath, surprised at the depth of his emotion. He was angry, yes, but it wasn't just anger. It was…it was…

Concern. Worry. Pain.

It'd hurt him when she left. It *hurt* that she'd walk away from him.

It crossed his mind that everything had changed. Something had happened in the past few weeks. Something had happened just yesterday. And something had happened today when he pressed her against the bedroom wall and felt her shudder beneath him, felt her body arch against him. He wasn't indifferent to her. Not in the least.

"Why did you run away yesterday?" he asked

abruptly, recognizing how heavily the question had been weighing on him the past twenty-four hours.

"Why did you ask me to marry you?"

"You already know that answer."

Her head lifted, her light brown ponytail swishing as she looked up at him. "I wouldn't have asked if I knew."

This was a new Winnie. A stronger Winnie, a more confident Winnie.

Certainly a more direct Winnie.

"Because you were the best candidate for the job," he answered lightly, trying for humor, but she didn't smile. Her grim expression didn't change.

"What about Annika?"

"What about Annika?" he retorted.

"Well, she's blond and beautiful and famous. She's your Swedish supermodel and she'd have looked perfect in the paper's page six photos."

"But I don't want to be the center of the society page. I don't want to spend the rest of my life photographed. I just want to live a normal life. A quiet life. A life away from the limelight."

It took Winnie a moment for the implications to hit her. She grit her teeth thinking he had incredible nerve. He didn't want a beautiful supermodel for a wife because the press would eat it up, but he'd marry her, a chunky little secretary who'd bore the media to death.

Her stomach physically hurt. "What about love?"

"I don't love Annika."

"You don't love me."

He didn't answer. The rawness inside her chest was

nearly intolerable. "You don't love me," she repeated, her tone turning savage. "Do you?"

Morgan regarded her steadily. "No."

"So why me? Why did you ask me?"

"You're different." His shoulders shifted. "You know me. You wouldn't be operating under some false romantic illusion about married life."

Because a woman like Winnie wouldn't have any romantic illusions. A woman like Winnie was practical, dependable, sensible. A woman like Winnie didn't get many offers and she ought to know that Morgan Grady wasn't just a good catch, but a dream catch.

God help her, but she was supposed to be flattered. He expected her to be *pleased*.

For the first time since working for him she thought she could actually hate him. He really had no idea who she was.

She'd waited her whole life for the magic of falling in love, for the chance to be deeply loved. Her sisters had been loved, adored, spoiled. Winnie wanted the same thing, too, but didn't think she'd ever have it…didn't think she deserved it until yesterday when she looked in the mirror at the expensive Park Avenue salon and saw what the bevy of makeup artists and hair stylists had done, saw how they'd turned her from stodgy Winnie Graham into someone utterly magical, truly beautiful.

Winnie had looked in the mirror, contact lenses in, hair glossed and pinned, makeup expertly applied and she'd seen a woman who deserved real happiness, a woman still longing for the fairy-tale ending. And a marriage of convenience wasn't even close to her idea of a happy-ever-after dream.

Yes, she'd have money, Morgan had ensured she'd be handsomely compensated, but what was money without love?

What was anything without love?

Winnie turned away and looked out toward the ocean. The late-afternoon sun shone hot and bright, glazing the beach.

"You know they're wrong," she said quietly, "those gossip columnists who called me a gold digger. I'm not interested in your money. I've never been interested in money—least of all yours."

She shook her head once, remembering the harsh things written about her in the past couple weeks and then looked back at him over her shoulder. Her lips twisted in a brief, rueful smile. "The only one thing I want from you is love."

CHAPTER EIGHT

MORGAN laughed. It wasn't a loud laugh, or harsh, but it was definitely laughter and it was the last thing Winnie expected to hear from him. "Why are you laughing?"

"Because you…you're…a dreamer."

"What's wrong with that?"

"Nothing, except you're bound to be disappointed, and you think you agreed to marry me for love—which is very virtuous—but it's not exactly the truth."

She stiffened, blood draining from her face. "You can't say that. You don't know that. You don't know me."

Morgan smiled grimly. "Actually, I'm beginning to know you. I'm starting to understand you. You're not quite the altruistic person you think you are. You might tell yourself that all you want from me is love, but that's not true. You want a lot more than that."

"Really?" She glared at him, temper rising.

"Really." He walked toward her. "You want passion, sex, glamour, adventure. You want to try something different, be someone different. You think with me it could happen, and you're right, it could. With me you can be anyone and anything you want to be—including yourself."

He stood just a foot away and Winnie had to tilt her head back to see his face. His eyes were narrowed, his expression closed, but the heat he was generating more than made up for his lack of expression.

Winnie was powerfully reminded of how it'd felt in his arms, pressed against his hard body. She felt the warmth increase now, and the slow, seductive rise in energy.

From the dark blue of his eyes, and the angle of his jaw, she realized he was feeling the change in tension, too.

"Neither of us are altruistic people, Winnie." He lifted a hand, touched the curve of her ear, rubbed his fingers lightly across the skin. His eyes met hers and held. "We both have needs—and some of these needs have nothing to do with love."

Winnie's pulse raced. His touch was amazing. He made her feel so many incredible things but her attraction to him was based on love, not lust. "Maybe you can reduce it to the physical, but I can't. I feel this way around you because I love you, not because you turn me on."

He smiled. "You're such a romantic. You want it all—love with a capital L, romance with a capital R, passion with a capital P—"

"Yes, I do, and I think it exists."

His smile reached his eyes. He had the most beautiful eyes, the most lovely shade of blue. They were the kind of blue one would never get tired of. Not a shiny plastic blue, but rich and dark, like sapphires and midnight and silk from the Far East.

His fingertips trailed down her neck. "We could be happy together, Winnie. I know I could make you happy."

His touch did one thing to her. His words did another. She felt her heart squeeze, protesting against his logic, and his cool pragmatic reasoning. "I couldn't ever be happy with you if I knew you didn't love me."

"There's all kinds of love. You're talking romantic love. I'm talking reality love. I'm talking respect, admiration, friendship—"

"Not that again!" she interrupted, drawing swiftly away.

She wanted passion, romance, love and he wanted respect, admiration, and friendship. How perfect was that?

Snorting to herself, Winnie reached for her frosty glass and took a swallow. He'd spent the last fifteen years dating models, actresses, socialites, but he wanted to marry her based on the incredibly dull virtues of respect and admiration.

He wanted to marry someone safe. Someone dependable. Someone dumpy, dowdy, dull.

"Boring!" she snapped, setting her drink down again. "I can't spend the rest of my life with a man who feels nothing for me—"

"But I do like you."

"*Like?* Morgan, I want *love.*" She was getting angrier. She needed to take a step back, calm down, but she was too irritated. "I want someone who really wants me, someone who can't keep his hands off me, someone who'd walk to the ends of the earth for me. I want the real thing, and that includes fireworks, amazing sex, and eternal love."

She felt his gaze but he didn't speak. Her shoulders slumped, anger fading. She drew a shaky breath. "I just don't want to settle for less. It'd be wrong to settle for less."

"And what if your idea of love doesn't exist?"

Her eyes burned and she blinked hard. "You're so cynical."

"Maybe. Or maybe I'm just a realist."

Maybe.

She blinked again, thinking that maybe it was possible to see life from two different perspectives, and have both be equally right. And if that was the case, while they'd never see eye to eye, it didn't mean they couldn't enjoy the moment and, let's face it, they were in the middle of paradise.

St. Jermaine's was the most beautiful place she'd ever been and from the looks of it, there'd be a gorgeous sunset later tonight. She was drinking her first banana daiquiri and soon she'd be sitting down to dinner with the love of her life.

Dinner was served on the veranda, white gardenias in a bowl, the glass table glowing with the flicker of a dozen white candles. It was the most romantic table she'd ever seen.

The service was discreet. Mr. Foley uncorked a bottle of red wine and disappeared. Morgan was being his charming best. Winnie leaned back in her chair and listened to the soft lap of waves against the sand.

I could get used to this, she thought, picking up her goblet, admiring the wine's ruby sheen. This is definitely the good life. Wouldn't it be something to really live like this? What would it be like to be Morgan's girlfriend...or his mistress?

"You're smiling," Morgan said, topping off her glass with more wine before refilling his own.

"I am," she agreed, stretching a little, very relaxed. She lifted her glass in front of one candle and let the flame glow through the goblet, marveling at the warm garnet glow, red symbolizing love...passion.

Sex.

Maybe it was the Merlot in her veins, or the balmy evening, but she felt really lazy and really happy, and swirling her glass, Winnie thought she'd like to feel this way more often.

To feel like this not just now, but always.

"What are you thinking?" Morgan asked, his dark hair gleaming in the candlelight, his teeth flashing.

She looked at him from beneath her lashes. "That you're not bad company when you're not worrying about the stock market."

He grimaced. "I don't worry about the stock market."

"No, you obsess about it."

Lines deepened near his mouth. He was trying not to laugh. "I'd never obsess about anything."

Her eyebrows arched.

He laughed out loud. "I must say, you're not bad company when you let your hair down." His dark blue gaze met hers, held. "I like your hair down."

"Literally or figuratively?"

His eyes were doing something crazy to her insides. Her heart raced and her arms felt weak, as if the bones had turned to butter. She slipped her hands to her lap and balled her fingers together.

"Both," he answered. "Don't pin it up anymore. I

like it down. I like you like this. You're an interesting woman, Winnie. You're constantly surprising me."

His compliment touched her. She felt a lump grow in her throat. "You like interesting women?" she asked, voice suddenly husky.

"Of course. Why, do you prefer boring men?"

She was feeling so much intense emotion she didn't think she had a laugh in her just then, but he'd found it and she chuckled. "Boring men, please."

"Good. I'm just your type. I'm very boring. Incredibly dull. You'll yawn yourself silly with me."

Her eyes locked with his, and his eyes were saying he wanted her. His eyes were making her feel hot and hungry again.

Blood rushed through her, from her middle up her neck, into her cheeks.

"We could have fun boring each other, Winnie." His voice was pitched so low it felt like velvet sliding across her skin.

"Yes."

"There's a lot of ways I could bore you."

Heat flooded her limbs yet again, and Winnie grabbed her water glass, took a big gulp. She'd like to be bored, if that's what he wanted to call it. She'd love to be bored as a matter of fact. "But I'm really not your type."

"What's my type?"

Winnie slowly looked up into his face. His eyes, so blue, so intense, were looking straight into hers. "Annika, Birget, Hannah—"

"Oh, yes, my blond Scandinavian supermodel type."

"It's true. It's your preference. You're attracted to tall, slender, sexy and that's certainly not me."

"No, you're not tall, and blond, but I'm still very attracted to you."

"Morgan, I don't think you understand me. I'm talking attracted as in sex."

Creases fanned from his eyes. "Winnie, I understand you perfectly. I'm talking about sex, too, and I think we'd have great sex together."

The warmth in her tummy did a sinuous dance through her middle, along her tense spine, flooding her quivery limbs with heat. Part of her brain told her she should drop the subject, back away from it now, but another part wouldn't let her. She was fascinated, intrigued by all that she didn't know and had never done. "You do? And how do you know?"

He shrugged. "I can tell from the way you kiss."

She felt hot all the way through, her skin scorching, pulse racing. She drew a breath but she wasn't getting much air. She was thinking about sex. Thinking about his mouth on her skin. "You liked the way I kiss?"

"And taste."

Winnie sagged against the back of her teak dining chair, heart thumping, belly clenching, aching in places she didn't think could ache.

His words made her want and his voice made her need and she thought she'd do just about anything if he'd teach her a few things about sex and passion and love. Or just sex and passion because she already had the love part figured out.

If he didn't insist on marriage, she could almost

imagine a life with him. There'd be dates, dinners, evenings out and evenings in.

Winnie could see herself riding down Park Avenue in his stretch limo, stepping out at one of the hot clubs, treated to a private box at the opera.

He'd have seats behind home plate at Yankee Stadium. There'd be ice skating at Rockefeller Square. She'd receive invitations to all the fashion premieres.

Stylish haircuts, waxed eyebrows, year-round tan—

The fantasy came to an abrupt end. Because even tan and waxed and wearing a stylish new do, she'd never feel complete, it'd never be enough if he didn't love her.

"It wouldn't work," she said after a moment, the lovely vision bursting like a bubble inside her head. "We wouldn't survive a week."

"Why not?"

"Look at us. You're…you…and I'm…me."

He laughed softly. "Very insightful."

"I'm serious."

"So am I. There's a lot of chemistry here, Winnie, more chemistry than I ever felt with Birget, or Hannah, or Annika."

Her head jerked up. She stared at him wide-eyed. "Really?"

"Really." He pushed aside his wineglass and stood up. "Let's head down to the beach to catch the sunset."

The sun was just setting when they reached the cove and the colors at dusk were incredibly intense—blood-red, bright orange, purple and turquoise water.

Winnie slipped off her sandals to walk barefoot through the surf and when Morgan threw himself down on the beach, she sat down next to him, burying her feet beneath the still-warm sand.

It was so quiet on his island. The birds she'd heard earlier were silent and unlike New York, which was never still, here there was nothing of civilization to disturb the peace. No voices, no cars, no traffic, nothing but the gentle lap of waves against the creamy edge of sand.

"It's lovely," she whispered, pressing her hands against the sand, feeling the warm soft grains against her skin.

Morgan nodded. "I feel good here. I feel calm here. And I like having you here with me."

She leaned forward and propped her chin on her forearm, not knowing what to say. She was still rather intimidated by him, still felt some awe that she was here, in the Bahamas, on Morgan's island. It was surreal. Intimate. Exclusive. It was almost as if she'd gone on the honeymoon even though she'd missed the wedding.

Morgan stretched out an arm, pointed to the water. "Look, the sun's going quickly now."

He was right. Once the round red sun hit the horizon, it sank fast, disappearing into ocean as if it were a heavy fireball, and for one exquisite moment the ocean lit up and the surface shone ruby and gold.

Winnie held her breath the last few seconds, feeling almost bereft when the sun disappeared altogether, leaving the horizon a quiet, sullen, blue.

"That was beautiful," she said, wrapping her arms more tightly around her knees. It was still warm out but the contrast between the intense red sky and the now gray night made her shiver.

Morgan must have noted her shiver because he reached over, touched the middle of her back. "Cold?"

"No." But she shivered yet again, not from cold as much as desire. When he touched her she felt so much, it was almost too much. She'd never known such pleasure.

For seven months now she'd battled her feelings. For seven months she'd tried to dismantle the desire, deny the need, ignore the want. She'd told herself her feelings would fade. She'd forced herself to go elsewhere, look for another job just to put distance between her and heartbreak but here she was at the end of July and she was still hoping, wanting, needing, dreaming.

Would it be so awful to stop fighting herself, to stop fighting for the higher, moral ground and to just let herself enjoy him? To just enjoy this?

Would it be so bad to be with him just for the moment and to take what she could…even if it was only sex?

"Winnie, we don't have to make any big decisions today."

She turned her head, looked at him, wondered how he could know exactly what she was thinking. "I used to believe I was really old-fashioned," she said, her throat so dry it felt as if she'd swallowed a bucket of sand. "But I'm beginning to think I'm not so very conservative."

"Winnie—"

"I don't want to marry you. If a marriage is to last it must be built on love, but there are things I'm curious about, and there are things I don't know."

He waited and she clenched her hands together, praying for courage. "I'd like if it you…" She drew a deep breath, finding these words almost impossible to say. "If you could teach me these things…show me how it works…what to do."

"You make it sound like rocket science."

"It is if you don't know how."

"Well, I don't think you need to worry. You're a natural." His lips slowly curved but the smile didn't reach his eyes. "It'll be easier than you think."

She loved it when he looked at her like that. When his eyes were serious, but she could feel the heat. He tried to check the emotion yet she felt it anyway. "That's what you said about kissing," she said a bit breathlessly.

Grooves formed next to his mouth. "And was I wrong about that?"

He was doing it again. Making her hot, making her want. Winnie exhaled slowly in the semidarkness, her skin so warm that she wanted to peel her camisole top off, push her skirt down and throw herself into the ocean.

And Winnie realized that's exactly what she wanted to do. Strip down. Get naked. Skinny-dip. She'd never done anything half so daring but this was the time, this was the night. If she didn't do something risky now, she never would.

"Want to swim?" she asked, blushing a little.

"You mean get our suits and head to the pool?"

"No." Her blush deepened, her face felt sensitive, and she thought that she'd do just about anything to make him kiss her soon. "Let's swim here." Winnie swallowed hard. "Naked."

Morgan scooped up a handful of sand and held it in his closed fist. He wasn't sure that stripping to skin and swimming was the thing he needed right now.

Winnie was having a really potent effect on him. He could feel her, smell her, still taste her. He'd been battling his desire all evening. Dinner had been a lesson in discipline. During the meal when she'd leaned forward and placed a hand on his forearm, he'd hardened instantly. Ardently.

It was one thing to hide an erection seated at the dinner table. It was another naked on the beach.

"Come on, Morgan," she entreated, leaning forward, her breasts brushing his bicep. Waves crashed not far from their feet, the salty spray coating their skin. "Swim with me."

He searched her face. She looked so eager, her face very alive, eyes wide, lips parted, her expression completely unguarded. He loved that about her—her openness, her freshness.

Beautiful women were always interested in protecting power, jostling for position. Annika had always kept her guard up. Hannah wouldn't ever compromise. Birget played coy. But not Winnie, and he thought she was just as beautiful, if not more beautiful, than the others.

He glanced behind him at his low house with the steeply pitched roof. It glowed like a mysterious Japanese lantern on a hill. The tiki torches lining the dirt path from the beach to the bungalow shimmered, yellow flames dancing and licking at the night. It was a warm night, warm enough to sleep outside, and definitely warm enough for a swim.

He opened his fingers and let the powdery sand slide through. "You really want to do this?"

"Yes," she answered, voice quavering.

"All right, but you go first."

CHAPTER NINE

"Go FIRST?" She'd risen and now stood above him, feet slightly apart and planted in the sand.

Her hands were on her hips and her shoulders were bare. She looked very sexy and he couldn't forget the softness of her mouth, the delicate shape of her lips, or the smoothness of her skin. Just thinking about the kiss, remembering the way she'd felt in his arms, made Morgan hard again.

He craved the feel of her. He longed to put his mouth against her collarbone, feel her gasp as his tongue traced the delicate skin at her throat and the hollow beneath her ear.

"Skinny-dipping was your idea," he reminded, wondering now how he could have ever thought her big or solid. She was barely five five, maybe five four.

Without a word Winnie reached behind her, unzipped her skirt and peeled the beige linen fabric over her hips, down her legs to fall at her feet. Morgan inhaled sharply as Winnie stepped out of the skirt, leaving her in just the beige camisole and the nude-colored panties.

Winnie had legs. Amazing legs that were smooth and silky and very bare.

She looked over her shoulder, at the water, giving him a glimpse of firm thighs and a rounded bottom. Morgan was turned on all over again. "I've never done this before," she said in a small, breathy voice.

Winnie, his Winnie, the Winnie he'd worked with for the past seven months was driving him absolutely crazy. "You're doing just fine."

Her lips curved briefly and grasping the edge of her linen camisole she pulled up, lifting it over her head.

As Winnie tugged the camisole up, Morgan caught the sway of full, firm breasts. The top came off and the rising moon flooded her with light, illuminating her pale soft skin. She wasn't wearing a bra. Her breasts swayed as she dropped the camisole onto the sand.

Blood surged through him. Blood pounded in his ears, in his limbs, in his groin and Morgan felt as if he'd been taken over, hit by a wave of hunger so strong he was a sixteen-year-old kid again, looking at a centerfold.

She was lushly made—full breasts, hips, thighs—the body of a woman as a woman was meant to be.

His desire stunned him. His body actually hurt.

This was Winnie. This was the woman he'd worked so closely with for seven and a half months and he'd never known how sexy, how seductive, how sensual she was.

"You're going to join me?" she asked, hesitating slightly, as if starting to doubt the wisdom of an evening swim.

"Yes." Morgan remained where he was but slowly began unbuttoning his white Egyptian cotton shirt. His fingers weren't quite steady. In fact, he could hardly concentrate on the task at hand, still too enthralled by the vision of Winnie.

If he hadn't promised to take things slow...

"You're having trouble with that last button," Winnie said, head tilted, watching him.

He looked down at his shirt. It was true. It was all unbuttoned but the last and his fingers couldn't seem to get it undone.

Winnie crouched in front of him. "Let me help," she said, crisply, impossibly matter-of-fact.

He stared at her breasts. They swayed just inches from his face. If he bent his head he could capture one of her pale pink nipples in his mouth.

Her nipple in his mouth. His tongue against the tiny round peak. His body surged. He ached. He ground his teeth together to keep from touching her now.

But oh, he wanted to taste her skin, wanted to feel her firm nipple in his mouth and he'd suck it, warm it, make her cry his name.

"This is a tricky button," she said, her voice breathless, her fingers brushing his bare stomach. His abdomen contracted, muscles tensing at her light touch.

He could imagine her fingers on him, could imagine her soft hands against his erection and he felt nothing like controlled logical Morgan Grady but another man altogether.

God, he wanted her. He wanted to touch her, taste her, discover her.

He hadn't felt this kind of hunger in years. He wanted his palms on her breasts, her nipple in his mouth. He wanted to slide his hands beneath the snug fleshtone panties and cup her bottom. He wanted to touch the satin span of thigh, the warmth between her legs, to make her as hot for him as he was for her.

"There, got it," she exclaimed, victorious. "Now maybe we can swim."

She stood up and took a step back, her breasts perfectly round. The moon bathed her in the most delicious white light and Winnie glowed from head to toe. Her hair shone, her skin looked luminous, her shape so wonderfully distinct that he felt like a primitive man wanting a cave, a fire, and his very own woman.

He could see her stretched out on a bearskin rug; picture her in a soft leather wrap that barely covered those amazing breasts. He'd peel the loincloth from her pale hips and kiss his way from her ankle bone to the moist silk above.

Morgan shook his shirt off and, standing, he unzipped his khakis, stepping out of them. Now it was Winnie's turn to covertly watch him and his erection grew harder, bigger; his whole body ached.

He saw her gaze drop to his white briefs. There was no way he could hide his attraction now.

She bit her lower lip, worried it a little and then her gaze lifted, back to his face. She looked thrilled and afraid all at the same time. "That just leaves the underwear."

Her husky voice just about did him in. Did she know the effect she had on him? Did she do this to everyone?

"My turn to go first," he said hoarsely, wondering when and how everything had changed on him. He'd wanted Winnie because he'd thought they'd have a simple relationship, an uncomplicated relationship, but what he was feeling now was far from simple or uncomplicated.

He wanted her, desired her, cared for her.

He *cared* for her.

Morgan swallowed. Everything was different. Everything was changing.

As he took off his briefs she slid her own panties off, bending over to step out of one leg and then the other.

Morgan groaned. She had the most shapely bottom, the fullest most gorgeous curve of breast he'd ever seen on a woman. In the twenty years he'd been sexually active, he'd never been turned on like this.

He felt so hard and tight and hungry that his muscles bunched, his heart raced, his groin felt hot and painful. He needed to get in the water fast.

Morgan dashed across the sand, waded thigh-deep into the water before diving under the surf. He swam a distance under the surface, arms pulling hard, feet kicking, trying to burn off some energy. The water wasn't cold but it felt significantly cooler than the fire raging inside his skin.

He was in trouble. St. Jermaine's was far removed from the world outside. St. Jermaine's made anything feel possible. Including keeping Winnie.

After a moment he swam an easy breaststroke back toward the beach. He met up with Winnie halfway. She was treading water, hair wet and slicked back, shoulders bare, globes of breast barely visible.

"Feels great out here," she said, arms drawing circles beneath the surface. "It's warmer than I expected, almost like bathwater."

And he could see himself taking a bath with her, bathing her. He could see himself spending a long, long time with her.

He floated next to her. "I've owned St. Jermaine's three and a half years and I've never done this before."

Winnie sank a little lower in the water, her chin disappearing. "Why not?"

"I don't know." He swam closer, lashes lowered as he studied her pale face in the moonlight. "It never felt right before."

Her lips curved. "And it's right now?"

It was right, he thought. At that moment, everything felt right. For much of his life he'd felt alone, distinctly cut off, but somehow with Winnie he never felt alone…or lonely. Something about her made sense to him. Winnie made sense. Even that wasn't rational or logical, simply a gut response. A heart response. *Instinct.*

And his instincts were never wrong.

The moon's reflection glinted off the water, back onto Winnie's oval face, gleaming shoulders, and pale skin.

He reached out, water running down his arm, and very gently touched her cheek. "Is it possible I've been waiting for you?"

She was staring straight at him. Her eyes were enormous. Her cheeks darkened, pink slowly staining her skin. "Morgan," she said his name softly, breathing shallowly.

Her eyes had turned very green, a sage green, and were growing darker by the moment. From the pink of her cheeks to her parted lips, he knew what she was feeling. He was feeling it, too. And he was having a damn hard time keeping his hunger in check.

"Morgan," she repeated.

Her sexy pitch turned him inside out. His body

strained. His head felt light. He'd never wanted anyone like this.

"Talk to me," she whispered, as she slowly, tentatively, reached out to touch him beneath the water and her hand brushed his thigh.

Heat shot through him as her fingers glided over his leg. Hot, sharp heat, and his body tightened all over again, fresh blood surging. He was close to exploding with pleasure and pain. Stifling a groan, Morgan wrapped a hand around her upper arm and pulled her toward him, water swirling between them.

He hooked a leg around her leg, braced her against his chest, his hands encircling her waist. The water was cool but she was warm. She drew a deep shuddering breath and he could feel her tummy convulse, ribs expanding.

She'd be lovely beneath him. Lovely on top of him. Lovely every which way known to man.

He drew her even closer, her wet soft breasts crushed against his chest, her nipples pebbled and grazing his own. He wanted to be inside her. He needed her mouth, needed her wet, needed her open.

She made a soft whimpering sound as his palm cupped her breast, his fingertips massaging the nipple. "Oh, Morgan—"

"You're beautiful, Winnie. You're the most beautiful woman I've ever known."

Tears filled her eyes and she pressed her hands against his shoulders. "Don't say that. You don't have to say that."

"It's true."

"Annika—"

"Nothing compared to you," he murmured, sliding his palm up, over the peak of her breast to her collarbone and down again.

Then he couldn't stand it a minute longer. He had to have her, had to taste her and his head descended, mouth capturing hers.

She tasted cool and hot, salty and sweet, and beneath the pressure of his lips she whimpered, her hands moving, caressing his shoulders, his chest, his back, his triceps. It was as if she couldn't get enough and he couldn't get close enough and water splashed and swirled around them as their legs twined below the surface, hip pressed frantically to hip.

"Do you want to go in?" she mouthed against his ear, her hands at his nape, fingers in his hair.

He loved the way she touched him, loved everything about being with her. "A little way in," he said, and turning onto his side, he swam closer to shore, carrying her along with him.

Once he could feel the sandy floor, and stand with ease, he lifted Winnie up, parted her legs and brought her close against him. He wrapped her legs around his waist and he cupped her below the water, her smooth round cheeks fitting perfectly in his hands.

She gasped as he caressed the curve of her backside, fingers stroking out and then in until he found the very hot soft part of her.

"Morgan," she choked, wriggling against him, "I don't know about this."

He felt the delicate shape of her, the petal-like lips, the tiny hooded nerve. "You don't like this?"

Like? Winnie thought, burying her face against

Morgan's damp warm shoulder, desperate to get even closer. What was there not to like? She felt wild, her senses taut, her nerves screaming. He was making her feel desperate desires. She wanted him to touch her. She wanted him to do everything to her. "I think I like it too much," she answered, her lips pressed to his neck, his skin warm and fragrant.

"I don't know if that's possible, not if you care about the person you're with."

He was touching her in such a way she couldn't think, touching her in a way that made her breath fast and shallow. His fingers played against her, played her and she felt almost helpless in his hands. "Oh, I care about the person I'm with," she murmured, feeling so much love just then.

"Good, then you can relax."

His touch was even more intimate now, his fingers slipping inside her. Winnie's thighs tensed and she wrapped her arms around his shoulders, her lips parting against the base of his throat. She'd imagined having sex but never imagined anything as seductive as this.

His fingers inside her made her ache for more of this, more of him. She writhed and he stroked her slowly, deeply and the pleasure was so intense she felt close to tears.

"Beach," she choked, practically grinding her hips against him. "Let's…go…to beach."

He carried her up in his arms and she was totally without inhibitions now. It seemed right to be naked and hot and craving each other.

On the beach they discovered a blanket, a stack of

towels and two terry-cloth robes. Their scattered clothes had been discreetly removed.

"Mr. Foley," Morgan muttered, shaking his head.

"He's very attentive," Winnie said, smiling a little, fighting the nervous urge to giggle.

"Another sign that Mr. Foley likes you." Morgan lowered her down to the quilted blanket. "He's good with details, but this is a first."

The blanket felt warm, the sand was soft and inviting. Winnie felt comfortable and deliciously languid. "I think like is too strong of a word."

He knelt next to her. "He was certainly concerned when I returned from the wedding without you."

She was about to answer when he ran a hand up the inside of her thigh, his hand returning to her inner heat. She closed her eyes, sucked in air, and thought she must be a hedonist because she'd never felt anything half so good and couldn't imagine anything ever feeling better.

Morgan shifted, parted her knees wider, lowered his body between. Before she fully understood what he intended to do, his mouth replaced his hand, his tongue substituting for his fingers.

Winnie gripped the blanket, squeezed the quilted cotton in her fists to keep from crying out loud. The intense sensation overwhelmed her. Okay, she thought, trying to catch her breath, this felt even better than the other.

He was doing something with his hand and his mouth, creating a pattern of feeling, a rhythm within her. She tried to make sense of the tightness coiling in her middle, her belly clenching, her legs beginning to tremble.

Without changing position, without shifting focus or

losing tempo, Morgan placed a palm on her tummy just above her pubic bone. The pressure of his hand coupled with the rhythm of his tongue was quickly building tension, layering sensation on top of sensation like children's blocks stacking all the way up, past the coconut trees to the starlit sky itself.

"But wait," she said, her voice raspy in the night, "I want you with me."

He kissed the inside of her thigh. "I'm with you."

"But I want it different for my first time, I want you in me."

"You might not be able to come. It can be hard for women—"

"I don't care. It doesn't matter." She reached down, ran her hand across his upper back, his muscles so beautifully hard, his skin silky smooth. "I'd rather feel you inside me...if that's okay with you."

He didn't say anything. He didn't have to say anything. Morgan shifted, braced himself on his elbows, stretching out over her.

With his knees he pressed her legs up and wide. His body touched hers. She could feel the tip of him and she sighed. Morgan caught her hands in his, and even as he lifted her arms up, over her head, he thrust smoothly into her.

Winnie sighed, tightening around him. His hands pressed against hers. He thrust harder, now a little deeper, then briefly stopped. "Are you okay?" he asked, buried all the way in her.

She couldn't help smiling. Okay? She felt perfect, fantastic. "Yes, oh, yes."

But he was still concerned. "I don't want to hurt you."

"You're not, you couldn't, you feel wonderful. Besides, I was ready for you."

She felt him smile against her neck, then he kissed her most tenderly on the sensitive place near her ear. "I have to agree with you on that."

What followed was without time, without definition, without words. He was with her, so completely with her that she no longer knew him from her. He touched her and moved with her so that it felt as if they were part of the air, the earth, the sky. Beautiful, Winnie thought, I feel really truly beautiful.

She gave in to him and the rightness of being together. She gave in to the warmth, the touch, the exquisite pleasure. It was thrilling being so close, healing, too. The energy was intense, the heat formidable. To be held like this, touched like this, loved like this.

Loved.

Morgan rolled over, drawing Winnie on top of him. She felt naked for a moment, and stiffened. But Morgan caressed her breast and drew her head down and kissed her. "Don't stop moving," he whispered, lips brushing hers. "You'll like this, I promise."

She wasn't sure, and she felt a little awkward but Morgan clasped her hips and shifted her a little and suddenly it all made sense. The heat was back, the tension building. The self-consciousness receded, the strangeness disappeared. She was his again. He was hers. They were together, neither was distinct, and as she moved against him light flashed against her closed eyes. Hot liquid sun, hot summer sun, red hot, so hot, and Morgan held her tighter, moved her faster. Winnie didn't think she could stand it, the tension growing, her muscles clenching, but he wouldn't let her escape.

"Morgan—" she choked, the heat so great, her skin so hot, beads of moisture forming everywhere.

He rose up to meet her, driving hard, fierce, and she couldn't contain it any longer, couldn't control it and with a cry she felt launched into the sun. Waves of light and heat rolled through her, waves of light and heat and pleasure until she shuddered from head to toe.

"I can't hold on much longer," he said, voice hoarse, muscles knotted hard.

"Then don't."

He lifted her off him, drew her down to his side. Groaning, he held her as he came.

Winnie waited a moment before gently touching his face. "You didn't have to pull out."

He leaned on his elbow and looked down at her, his expression gentle, rueful. He pushed back a damp lock of hair from her forehead and kissed her warm brow. "Yes I did. I really wanted to be in you, but it wouldn't be fair. I'm not about to trap you into marriage."

She stared up at him, into his eyes. His black lashes were so thick they cast shadows on his face. "You've changed your mind about marrying me?"

He pulled her back on top of him, slid a hand up the length of her back. "Not at all, sweetheart, but I think you need to live a little first."

His lips were creating havoc on her skin. His hands were tracing the shape of her spine. Her body was stirring to life again. How could he still make her feel so much? Want so much?

"Live a little?" she gasped as he drew her nipple in his mouth. The warm wet feel of his mouth, the pointed flick of his tongue was driving her crazy, making her need and want and ache. Her breast ached. Between her legs ached. She was dying to feel him inside her again.

"Live," he said, his breath fanning her wet breast. "Experiment. Do all the things you've always dreamed of doing."

"I think…I think…" she said, voice breathy, faint, as he flipped her over onto her back and parted her knees with his own.

He smoothed the hair back from her face and trailed his hand from her breast to her belly and back to her breast again, his touch light, tantalizing, maddening. "Yes?"

"I think I'm…" She exhaled as he entered her again, his body so hard, his tension barely leashed. "…doing them."

And it was, she thought, as he filled her body, and filled her heart, the most beautiful experience she'd ever known. The reality of making love to Morgan was far better than anything in her wildest imagination.

CHAPTER TEN

LATER they put the robes to good use, wrapped themselves in the plush terry-cloth, and walked back to the house.

It was well past midnight, and Winnie stumbled a bit on the dirt path, the tiki torches burning so low that several had burned themselves out.

Morgan touched her elbow, steadying her as they reached the stone steps leading from the lower terrace to the house.

She smiled her thanks, so calm she didn't need words. Talking seemed redundant after all that had taken place. It had been the most amazing, perfect night. She knew she might not ever experience a night like this again, knew that the intensity, the chemistry and the passion she'd felt were unique to being with him.

Winnie didn't need to be told that not everyone clicked like this. She didn't need a dozen partners to recognize that what she'd found, what she'd felt, was something few people ever knew. Somehow she had been blessed. Somehow she'd been one of the lucky ones.

The house was quiet, most of the interior lights dimmed. Here and there a small light illuminated a work of art, and some of the large bronze sculptures. But lights were unnecessary with the windows unshuttered and the moonlight pooling in. The house felt like an extension of the warm sultry night and Winnie held her breath a moment, telling herself to remember, telling herself to forget nothing.

This is a taste of heaven, she thought, holding her breath a moment, keeping the joy within. To be loved like this. To be touched like this. To feel so good, so amazing with someone else.

Morgan brushed her elbow, prompting her forward, directing her past the dining room to the kitchen. In the kitchen a light glowed above the large French stove, the stove painted a cheery color red. "Hungry?" he asked.

She nodded. "And thirsty."

"Grab one of the bar stools."

Winnie sat at the counter, discovering that sitting she was more tender than standing. Definitely no longer a virgin. Thanks to Morgan she knew a great deal more than she had this time yesterday.

Morgan foraged in the huge stainless-steel refrigerator, gathering fruit and cheese and bottles of chilled mineral water.

He carried everything to the counter, before locating a loaf of bread, butter and a sharp knife.

It was like a picnic, sitting at the counter in the virtual dark. They ate bread and cheese, and while Morgan cut juicy slices of mango and papaya, he didn't talk.

She was glad; words would spoil it. Winnie liked the silence, the stillness, and the sense of mystery.

Until tonight she'd never really lived. Until tonight she'd never fit her skin. She'd always felt so plain before, so heavy and awkward, but in Morgan's arms and against Morgan's chest she felt lovely. Lovely on the inside as well as the out.

No longer a girl, but now a woman.

There are certain rites of adulthood and tonight she'd been initiated into the most meaningful of all.

It wasn't about sex, she thought, sucking the juice from a papaya slice, but about living. It was one thing to love a man with your heart, but something entirely different to love him with your soul.

She loved Morgan through and through, and making love had only deepened her trust, cemented her loyalty. No matter what happened in the future, she would always be part of him, and he'd be part of her.

Satiated in more ways than one, Winnie yawned. She tried to cover her mouth with her hand but Morgan still caught the yawn and laughed softly.

"You're beat," he said, handing her a damp paper towel to wipe her sticky fingers clean.

"I am beat," she admitted, scrubbing the juice from her fingers and the palm of her hand.

He watched her for a moment before leaning forward and kissing her on the forehead, then on her mouth. "Thank you."

Winnie set the crumpled paper towel down. "Why are you thanking me?"

"Because." His dark blue eyes looked almost black in the dim kitchen light.

Winnie waited, forcing him to articulate.

His smile was small, his eyes shadowed with things he still hadn't shared, stories and history he kept buried inside. "It was good tonight. It was really good between us. It just felt right."

It did.

It felt really right.

Warmth filled her. Her eyes burned, and the emotion she felt was so different from other happiness. This happiness was something permanent, something she'd always have because she'd had one perfect evening, one most perfect setting, and one most perfect lover. "I love you."

She hadn't meant to say it, had thought the words, had felt the words, but hadn't meant to say anything at all. But now that the words had been spoken, she didn't regret it. How could she? It was the truth, and if she couldn't be honest with him now, when could she?

Morgan held her face in his hands, his thumbs against the curve of her cheekbones. "Winnie, I believe in you." He kissed her mouth gently, in a long lingering kiss. And when he lifted his head he added, "Now it's time for you to believe in you."

He kissed her briefly and they said good night. Winnie closed the bathroom door behind her, turned on the shower, dropped her robe and stepped inside the wide white-marble enclosure. She let the hot water pulse down, rinsing all the salt and sand and perspiration away.

Hair clean, skin clean, Winnie toweled off, brushed her teeth, slathered lotion all over and climbed into bed.

But sleep was fitful. Hours later her body was still so sensitive that she'd wake, certain that Morgan was with her, that his hands were on her and they were making love again.

By the time morning came Winnie felt exhausted. She woke up at five, went to her window, folded the shutters back and pushed open the sliding French door. For nearly a half hour she sat on her balcony and listened to the waves roll and crash and felt the cool night air slowly warm.

She'd always believed that love was the most important thing between a man and a woman, and she'd promised herself years ago that she'd wait to make love until she was truly in love. Well, she'd done that. She'd waited to make love, she'd waited for Morgan, and last night proved that the wait had been worth it.

But what happens now?

She curled up in the chair and watched the sun begin to rise, the purple sky lightening to weak yellow and pale blue.

From her balcony she could see a strip of white sand and she thought of them last night, out there, in the water and on the beach. She could picture Morgan naked in the moonlight, his broad shoulders and chest a gorgeous sun-kissed shade of gold. She could still see him, the way he'd looked reclining on the blanket on the sand. He'd been passionate and yet gentle, confident and loving.

It'd been such an amazing experience. The dinner, the sunset, the late-night swim. These things didn't usually happen in her life. These were the kinds of story-book events that happened to other people—people like her sisters, people like Annika, people who were poised and sophisticated and physically beautiful.

Morgan had said last night he found her beautiful but that was last night in the heat of the moment. Would he find her beautiful later, when back in New York? Would he find her as sexy and compelling when life returned to normal?

Winnie stirred restlessly, uncomfortable with the

questions she posed to herself. She didn't want to answer those questions, didn't want to think about the future.

She got out of her chair, left the balcony to return to her bed. She drew the sheet up, covered herself all the way to her chin as if she could somehow block the little voice of doubt already whispering in the back of her head.

Things here might feel idyllic but this is paradise. What happens when you leave heaven for Manhattan? What happens when you're back in the Tower's building and working for him?

It was after ten when she woke up again and this time she was more rested. Dressed in a light green sundress, Winnie wandered through the house, outside to the veranda and, hearing Morgan talk, she followed the sound of his voice.

As she descended the stairs to the pool terrace she caught snatches of his conversation.

"How can she be having trouble already?" Morgan said shortly. "I'm not even there. There shouldn't be anything stressful for her to *do*."

Winnie opened the wrought-iron gate and closed it behind her. As she rounded one large pot teaming with hibiscus flowers she spotted Morgan on the phone, pacing by the pool.

He wore nothing but navy cotton shorts, and his skin, burnished bronze, glistened. Winnie spotted a pair of shoes next to one of the chaise longues and realized he'd only just returned from a run.

"No!" he thundered, voice rising. "I shouldn't have to be dealing with this now. I'm on vacation."

He didn't know she was there, she realized, recognizing he was on a business call, probably with someone from the office. It was Monday morning and most people were back at work.

Morgan swore softly and raked a hand through his dark damp hair. "You're not listening," he interrupted sharply. "The whole point of hiring her was to ensure I didn't have to be doing this while I was gone. If she can't handle the job, get rid of her. I can't afford these kinds of mistakes."

This didn't sound good. Someone had clearly goofed at the office and she knew better than anyone that Morgan didn't tolerate sloppy work or thoughtless errors.

Morgan turned around and spotted her there. His brooding expression cleared and he lifted a hand, waving her over.

"Handle this," he concluded as she approached him. "Today." Without saying goodbye, he abruptly hung up.

Winnie dropped down on one of the chaise longues. "Did you have a good run?"

"Yes." He leaned over, kissed her. "Although I have to admit I'm not working at full strength."

She felt herself blush a little but she couldn't help grinning. "What happened? Too much exercise yesterday?"

"Not too much, just right." He moved to the freestanding shower set back from the pool, turned the faucets on and rinsed himself off.

Clean, he grabbed a towel from the pool cabana and rubbed his hair dry. Winnie didn't mean to stare but he was so beautifully made, so tightly constructed of muscle and bone.

Morgan sat down next to her. "Had breakfast yet?"

"No, but I'm not very hungry."

"Well, lunch won't be long now. Here on island time the kitchen's always open and there's always something good to eat."

"Island time. I like that." Leaning back she looked up into the azure sky. She could hear birds twittering and warbling. Sunshine glazed everything with perfect white-gold light. Life here was certainly far removed from the cares of New York.

From the worries of the office and the billions of dollars Morgan managed at Grady Investments. Which reminded her of Morgan's conversation. "Everything all right at the office?"

He sat forward, muscles in his hard abdomen contracting. "There are a couple of problems, but nothing that won't get straightened out."

"Sounds like an administrative problem," she cautiously persisted. "Something happen with one of the assistants?"

Morgan draped his towel around his neck, biceps bunching. "I might have to let someone go."

She mentally went through the administrative assistants that worked for Grady Investments. Most of them had been there for three years or more. "Who?"

"You don't need to worry—"

"But maybe I can help. Maybe when we get back I can put in some time, or help her on training. It could be that she's gotten rusty. I'll sit down with her first thing next Monday.''

He ruffled his hair. "It's not quite that easy. She's my new assistant.''

Winnie sat there stunned. For the longest moment she couldn't think of anything to say. She wasn't thinking period. Finally she roused herself and scooted to the edge of the longue, put her feet over the side as if she were bracing herself. "You fired me?"

"I didn't fire you.''

"But you have a new assistant.''

He didn't immediately speak. Then he exhaled slowly, a low rush of air. "Yes.''

She felt a rush of emotion, a very painful rush of emotion. "I can't believe you replaced me.''

"You were marrying me.''

"But you *can't* replace me. I had a job. I liked my job. You can't replace me without discussing it with me.''

Morgan stood up, took a few steps and snapped his towel. "We were getting married, Winnie. I thought you'd have enough to do at home—''

"What?" she demanded, jumping to her feet. "Ironing? Cooking? Grocery shopping?''

"No, I have Mr. Foley for all that,'' he answered impatiently.

"Exactly! If we'd gotten married, what would I do all day?''

Morgan groaned. "I don't want to do this. I want breakfast and coffee. I'm on vacation. Island time. No fights here, no rules, either.''

"No!" Her eyes burned. A lump filled her throat.

"You can't dismiss the conversation, or me, like this. You've taken my job from me, and I loved my job—"

"You couldn't have loved it that much. You were looking for a new job. You flew to Charleston just five weeks ago and interviewed with Osborne Manufacturing."

Winnie felt a heaviness settle in the pit of her stomach and she blinked hard to keep the tears from falling. "When did your new assistant start?"

"Winnie."

"Tell me!"

"Today."

"When were you going to tell me?"

"We were going to be on our honeymoon. I needed someone at the office. You can't be in two places at once."

She shook her head, hurt and furious. "Well, then I take the job!"

"Bull." He crossed the flagstones, walking to her. "You didn't like the job. You liked being with me."

"Wrong."

He caught her by the waist, dragged her toward him. "Not wrong. I know you," he said, voice deepening. "Maybe you did like your job, but you love me more. You want me more."

His mouth covered hers in a hard, relentless kiss, his hands burying deep in her loose hair. His tongue parted her lips and he drank the air from her lungs. Winnie's head swam, her senses reeling from the explosive contact.

He'd never kissed her like this before, never kissed her with anger or aggression, but she wasn't afraid as much as excited. His emotion matched her own and she answered his kiss, boldly pressing herself against him, and standing on tiptoe to cup the back of his head, her fingers coiling in his damp crisp hair.

She felt him harden against her, felt his arousal through his thin cotton shorts. He groaned deep in his throat as she rubbed her hips across him and with one hand he cupped her breast, kneading the nipple.

Winnie loved the feel of his hand on her breast and when he nudged her legs wider apart she wanted to be naked, wanted to feel him buried inside her.

"Come with me," he said, breaking away and leading her into the cool darkness of the poolside cabana.

He closed the door behind them, reached under Winnie's sundress and pulled off her panties and then hoisted her onto the slate counter.

The counter's coolness against her hot skin heightened her awareness.

He slid the spaghetti straps of her sundress off her shoulders and then pushed the thin green fabric down so that her dress wrapped around her waist.

"You're gorgeous," he said, bending his head to suck one nipple and then the other.

She was feeling so warm, very excited, yet he wouldn't touch her anywhere but on her breasts. Winnie battled to catch her breath as he alternately lashed and suckled each nipple with his tongue.

She squirmed on the counter, needing, wanting, and feeling completely empty. "Please."

He looked up at her, his jaw thick, his eyes dark with passion. "Please, what?"

"Touch me."

"But I am."

Heat burned in her cheeks. "No, you know."

He shook his head. "No, I don't know."

But he ruined his excellent acting by sliding his thumbs across her damp, sensitive nipples, creating fresh friction, more tension, more heat.

Winnie shuddered, rib cage expanding as she drew a deep unsteady breath. "Morgan—"

"Yes?"

His thumbs were drawing endless circles on the areolas. His thumbs went around and around, circles that made her belly clench and her insides ache and her knees clamp together to appease the urgent need.

She felt hot. Hot inside her skin. Hot outside her skin. She couldn't stand such bittersweet torment.

Morgan lifted her head forcing her to look deep into his eyes. "What do you want?" he persisted.

"You."

Without letting her go, he pulled her forward, parted her knees and entered her in one smooth, swift stroke. His thrusting was hard, intense, deliberate. He held her hips firmly and with each stroke buried himself more deeply. This was primitive and raw, fierce and possessive. Winnie knew she wouldn't be able to hold back much longer.

As she reached the point of no return Winnie whimpered, dug her hands into Morgan's shoulders and he covered her mouth with his, sucking her cry of pleasure into him.

This lovemaking was different from that of last night. Last night had been gentle, tender, beautiful. This lovemaking was just as intense, her orgasm had shattered her, but today she felt Morgan's drive, his expertise, his will.

It was as if Morgan was showing her how much she wanted him, just how much she needed him, and that *he* was the one firmly in control.

During the next few days they fell into a pattern of eating, playing and lovemaking. Some mornings they'd sail, other afternoons they'd snorkel, but inevitably they retreated from the world, stripped off their swimsuits and spent long hours immersed in a very private world of touch and pleasure.

Over the course of the week Winnie discovered how to touch Morgan and what turned him on. She loved making him hard, loved building the anticipation and loved it even better when she could answer his hunger. She learned to use her hands, her mouth, different positions with her body. It all felt so natural with him. Nothing ever felt wrong.

By the middle of the week Winnie had been moved into Morgan's bedroom. He said he couldn't stand waking up and not discovering her there and frequently he woke her when the sky was still dark and the night far from over but he'd already be hungry for her warmth, her softness and her skin.

One evening, curled up next to Morgan, their skin still damp from lovemaking, Winnie forced herself to return to the issue that had been bothering her since Monday. "What happens when we go home? What am I supposed to do if I don't have my job?"

His fingers lightly stroked her hip. "Move in with me."

She lifted her head a little, frowning. "I don't get it."

He shrugged. "I want you to live with me. Be with me. I'll take care of the bills."

For some reason his calmness struck her as indifference. Didn't he understand that work was important? That she got a sense of self-worth from working? That much of her self-esteem came from doing a great job?

Winnie rolled away from him and sat up on the edge of the mattress. "As much as I like sleeping with you, Morgan, that doesn't quite constitute a full-time job."

He folded his arms behind his head and looked at her. "We could make it a full-time job."

"This is important."

His expression hardened. "You knew when I proposed that I've had enough of the bachelor thing. I'm sick of being single. I like being with you. I like sleeping with you. I like waking up with you. So this is just as important to me. Move in with me. Make this a permanent relationship."

She drew an unsteady breath, shaken and more than a little confused. Was this his way of saying he loved her? "We're not married, Morgan."

"We don't have to be married to live together."

"But you don't love me."

"Winnie, I don't think I'll ever love anyone..."

"You loved Charlotte," she flashed, interrupting.

He swore. Angry. Really angry. "I learned my lesson. I don't fall in love anymore."

CHAPTER ELEVEN

HE LOVED Charlotte, but he didn't love her. He'd loved Charlotte, but he *wouldn't* love her. Winnie couldn't get the words out of her head and nothing was quite the same after that.

They stayed on the island for another three days and on the surface their physical relationship remained the same but there were new undercurrents between them, friction that hadn't been there before.

It was almost a bitter point for her that Morgan still brought her to the peak of pleasure, still applied his immense skill, but it wasn't a physical release she wanted as much as emotional.

Was this just sex? Would Morgan ever love her? And if it was just sex, wasn't it inevitable that he'd tire of her?

On their last evening on St. Jermaine's, Morgan went for a sail on his own and Winnie stood on her balcony studying the sky, and the horizon. Waiting for the sun to set for the last time.

Heart heavy, she watched the fiery red sun drop, seemingly disappearing into the middle of the ocean, and as the water exploded crimson and gold, tears filled her eyes.

Goodbye, paradise. She was ready to go home.

They reached New York late Sunday afternoon. Morgan had two cars waiting at the airport. One limousine was for Winnie, the other for himself and Mr. Foley.

So it's over, she thought, just like that. One week of great sex and then put the girl in the car and send her on her way.

As her limousine drove over bridges, on and off freeways, through tunnels, and past tollbooths, Winnie had plenty of time to think.

She wasn't entirely sure why Morgan had cooled toward her, but she knew why she'd cooled toward him. It wasn't just his job, or Charlotte, or Annika—it was his complete lack of emotional commitment.

No words of love. No promise of security. Just wink, wink, "I'll pay the bills as long as you continue to take care of me."

Maybe he didn't mean it exactly like that, but it's how it felt, and it felt rather sordid.

Oh, Winnie, she thought, closing her eyes, you didn't have a prayer. From the beginning you were in over your head. You can't substitute sex for love. You can have love without sex, but face it, you're a mush-head, a softie, a born romantic. You don't have a crush on Morgan, you're *in love*. And whatever game you've been playing lately is going to obliterate you.

The driver parked the limousine in front of her Upper West Side apartment building, and carried her suitcase to the door.

"I can manage from here," she said.

"Mr. Grady said I was to see you up."

Hot tears burned the back of her eyes. If only *Mr. Grady* had said something kind to her when they parted! If only he'd said, "Thanks for a great week. Take care of yourself. I'll be thinking about you.'' But not a word. Not a goddamn word.

She blinked hard. Her chest ached with emotion she was afraid to let out. "Tell Mr. Grady you had no choice,'' she said, taking her suitcase from the driver. "Tell Mr. Grady I refused to let you in.''

Her building didn't have a doorman and she jammed her key into the lock, opened the front door and closed it behind her.

She crossed the lobby, went to her mailbox and retrieved a week's worth of mail before taking the elevator up to her apartment on the eleventh floor.

Upstairs her footsteps were muffled as she walked the faded green carpet to her apartment at the very end of the corridor. Her apartment was a corner unit and the long silent walk seemed to last forever and each step made her feel even farther from Morgan. Damn him. Damn his beautiful, arrogant, egotistical hide!

By the time she reached her door the tears were falling in earnest. Shifting her suitcase and armful of mail, Winnie fished out her key yet again and leaned against her door to unlock the deadbolt. But as her shoulder hit her door, the door fell open.

Her apartment wasn't locked. The door wasn't even completely closed.

Someone had been here.

It seemed like forever as she stood there, trying to figure out what to do before she forced herself to take a step into her apartment and flick on the light.

With the light on, her heart fell.

Her apartment had been trashed. All her furniture had

been upended. Clothes lay in heaps. Broken glass glittered on the floor.

Winnie dropped her mail and suitcase and raced back to the elevator. She was running in slow motion, a raw physical terror stretching time out, distorting reality.

Wildly she punched the down button, begging it to return. Once downstairs, she called the building manager on the house phone. The building manager summoned the police and Winnie sat in the apartment lobby until the officers arrived.

It took the police nearly a half hour to make an appearance and even then they didn't seem overly concerned.

"This is New York," one of the officers said, heading upstairs to check out her apartment. "We can't respond to every break-in call as if it's a homicide."

"But what if the intruder's still up there? What if he's hiding somewhere?"

"Highly unlikely, but don't worry, we'll check it out, and I promise we'll let you know what we find."

Winnie spent another half hour alone in the lobby while the police did their work upstairs. Finally one of the officers returned to the lobby to take a statement from her.

After filling out the lengthy report, Winnie headed upstairs to inspect the actual damage. Maybe, she told herself, it wasn't as bad as it looked.

But walking into her tiny living room was still shocking. Whoever had been there had done quite a number. Almost everything had been turned over, emptied, or broken.

She didn't understand it. She had no money, no jewelry, no art, nothing of value and yet her apartment had virtually been destroyed.

The police left behind a copy of the report and form with a number where she could call periodically to check on her "case." But Winnie knew nothing would ever come of the "investigation."

Winnie did a slow walk around her apartment, wearily noting that whoever had been here had been very thorough. Her pillows were cut. Her mattress upended. All the clothes dumped from her closet.

What was the point? What did they want, and was it really necessary to slash her couch? Did the intruder honestly think she'd hidden a hoard of diamonds in her cheap sofa cushions?

"What the hell happened?" Morgan's voice thundered through Winnie's apartment.

Winnie jumped and shrieked, whether in fear or relief it was hard to say.

"Why didn't you call me?" he demanded, stripping off his blazer, dropping it on the back of her cushionless couch.

"I...I..." she looked at him, stuttering, utterly helpless. "I..."

"What?"

Her heart pounded. Her stomach churned. "I didn't think you'd care."

Morgan swore a string of violent epithets strong enough to make a hardened sailor blush. "What do you mean you don't think I'd care? I just spent the last week proving to you I care. If that doesn't say anything—"

Winnie's jaw dropped. "Say anything?" she interrupted hotly. "You never say anything. You make love and go to sleep. Make love and go to sleep."

His hands were on his hips. "But that should tell you something. I don't make love with someone I don't like."

"*Like?* I don't want to be liked. I want to be loved."

His eyebrows flattened, his expression as dark as Winnie had ever seen it. "For Pete's sake, woman, like, love, what's the difference? I want you. I wanted you with me. I asked you to move in with me. I told you I wanted to take care of you. But no, that wasn't good enough for you."

He was making it sound as if she'd been the unreasonable one. "You implied I'd be your *mistress!*"

"I thought you might like the idea."

"Like being your mistress?"

"Well, you sure didn't want to be my wife!" His dark blue gaze was as brittle and cold as black ice. "I'm just trying to figure out what you want, Winnie. You obviously don't want to be my mistress, you *really* don't want to be married to me, so what the hell *do* you want from me?"

Love. But that was the one thing he'd told her he couldn't give.

He could give her things, give her a name, give her pleasure, but he couldn't—wouldn't—give her love.

She bit her lip, fighting tears. "What are you doing here, anyway?"

Morgan snorted, walked away from her, picking his way around the mess but even as he walked she heard glass crunching beneath his shoes. "Your building manager called, let me know what had happened." He turned back, eyes snapping. "Because you sure weren't going to phone me."

Winnie slowly sat down again. He was angrier than she'd ever seen him. "How did my manager know to call you?"

He made a hoarse sound, jaw jutting all over again. "I can't believe you care about details like that at a time like this!"

She'd always thought he was so calm, so controlled, but there was nothing calm or controlled about him right now. He looked like a huge panther ready to pounce. He was stalking, growling, hissing. He wanted blood.

She swallowed, rubbed her hands on her knees. Her knees were cold. She felt chilled straight through. She'd worn a skirt and blouse on the plane, but despite the summer heat, she was freezing now. "I didn't know my building manager knew you."

Morgan muttered another unflattering word beneath his breath before marching back to her and pulling her up onto her feet. "I asked him to look out after you. I gave him money to keep an eye on you. I've been paying him since January if you really want to know."

"January?"

He grasped her upper arms, pulled her closer, head tipping so he was speaking very close to her mouth. "I worried about your neighborhood. I knew you didn't have family in the state, I thought you needed someone keeping an eye out for you. Okay?"

"Okay."

Any fight left in her was gone. She didn't know what to think at the moment and her emotions were scattered.

She was tired. She was hungry. She was overwhelmed, really overwhelmed.

He tipped her chin up, stared down into her eyes. "Don't you ever scare me like that again, do you understand?"

Winnie couldn't look away. She could see the navy of his eyes, the reflection of herself, and something else, too, something very dark and shadowed, something which made her think of long-buried pain.

"But I wasn't hurt, Morgan."

"That's not the point." A muscle popped in his jaw. "I told my driver to walk you up. I told him to check out the apartment first—" He broke off, teeth grinding together and, releasing her, he took a step away. For a long silent moment he did nothing but shake his head, a slow furious shake.

"You can't stay here tonight," he said at length. He glanced at his wristwatch, noting the late hour. "I'm going to call Mr. Foley and have him make up a room for you at my place."

The guest *room*, a voice silently taunted. *Not his room, but the* guest *room.*

"That's not necessary. I'll be all right here. It's just a mess. I'll start cleaning things up and it'll be fine by morning."

He snapped his fingers impatiently. "The lock's been jimmied. You need a locksmith. It has to be replaced. Or do you want to argue about that, too?"

He faced her. "Do you want to get anything? Is there anything you want to pack, anything you don't want to leave? This is your chance. Grab whatever you want because there might not be an opportunity to return."

Mr. Foley met them at the door of Morgan's Fifth Avenue apartment. Morgan's elegant apartment was one of the most coveted spaces in all of Manhattan.

"Are you all right, Miss Graham?" Mr. Foley asked, solicitously taking her travel bag and the stack of mail she'd brought with her.

"I think so."

"You need a hot bath and some dinner in bed." Mr. Foley's tone was very firm. "I've something in the oven for you, a delicious stuffed Cornish game hen and a lovely pear tart for dessert. Now if you'll follow me," he said, bowing slightly, "we'll get you settled for the night."

Morgan watched Mr. Foley usher Winnie away as if she were the most delicate, fragile being on the face of the earth. Well, she might be delicate, Morgan conceded, but she was also damn stubborn. Let Mr. Foley spoil her. His butler was obviously crazy about Winnie and Mr. Foley had never been crazy about anyone Morgan had dated before. In fact, Mr. Foley had never even *liked* anyone Morgan had dated before.

Frowning, Morgan went in a different direction, heading for his study. He'd only just started going through a week's worth of voice mails and business mail when he'd been notified that Winnie was in trouble.

Winnie. In trouble. Winnie. And trouble. Didn't those two just go together like peas in a pod?

Morgan tried to go through the rest of his voice mail but now he was too tired to concentrate. Heading for his bedroom, he showered, put on a pair of old cotton sweats for bed, but stopped short of turning in for the night.

He had to finish catching up. He forced himself to return to his study.

Leaning over his desk, Morgan flipped on the halogen lamp, and continued playing back the rest of his voice mail messages.

Family. Friend. Family. Sales call. Sailing buddy. Sales call. Morgan sighed, and really hated the phone. It was way too easy for people to leave a dozen messages, but it took forever for him to answer them all.

The next call stopped him cold. It was a voice from the past.

Hello, Morgan, Charlotte here. Darmouth Charlotte— He slowly lifted his head, eyes staring out across his office but seeing nothing. *I think we should talk… We need to talk. I've wanted to call you so many times but I dial your number and hang up before I ever leave a message.*

She drew a small breath and the sound of it was captured on the recording. Morgan's gut hurt. He held his breath waiting for her to finish.

I'm sorry about the wedding, our wedding, I mean. I've always been sorry, but maybe it's for the best. I don't know. Call me. Please. Soon as you can. She rattled off her number before hanging up.

Morgan scrawled the number on a tablet on his desk, numbly deleted the message and played the next.

The next call was from Winnie's parents and they were rather frantic about their daughter's whereabouts as they hadn't heard from her since the day after the wedding that didn't happen.

Mrs. Graham gave him a number where they were staying, said it was a vacation house they'd rented for a couple weeks in the mountains and asked him to make sure Winnie phoned as soon as possible.

Morgan wrote this one down, too, but his thoughts were chaotic and it wasn't until all messages were played, that he hung up the phone and really studied Charlotte's number.

For a long moment he didn't move. She'd called him. She wanted to see him.

He looked away, stared at the shadowed wall, but he could still hear her voice, imagine her face. Glacier blond, glacier beautiful. Impatient, imperious Charlotte.

He'd loved her so much. He'd loved her too much. He'd waited years to speak to her, years to hear from her, but now that she'd finally called, and now that he had her number, he wasn't sure he had anything to say to her.

Abruptly Morgan turned off the lamp on his desk. As a matter of fact, he was certain he had nothing to say to her.

Morgan did not sleep well that night. It had less to do with Charlotte's call than knowing Winnie was in his house, sleeping just down the hall.

He hated not sleeping with her. He hated not being with her. But he also hated not knowing what she wanted from him.

He was still wide awake two hours later when his bedroom door creaked open and he heard a timid voice say, "Who broke into my apartment? What did that person want?"

Morgan propped himself up. "I don't know."

She stood there in the shadows, hanging on to the doorknob, her long hair half hiding her face. "Mr. Foley said that it might have been someone who wanted to know about us. Someone curious about...you."

Morgan silently cursed taciturn Mr. Foley for finally speaking and definitely saying too much. "Maybe."

He heard her sniff. "You know, someone should tell the media that you're really not worth the trouble, and definitely not worth all this fuss." Her voice grew thinner, higher. She was close to breaking down. "People should know that you're not all that interesting, that you prefer numbers and mergers to love and affection, and that you proposed to me because I'm dependable and convenient."

He smiled despite himself and shook his head. She was such a handful. How could he have ever thought her easy, sensible, convenient? "Someone should tell them, and I think it should be you," he agreed, happy to pacify her. "However, it's three in the morning and not even the most tenacious journalist will be at his desk for another hour or two. So let's go back to bed and get some sleep."

But she didn't move. "I can't sleep. I'm scared."

He slid out of bed and walked across the room and gently but firmly closed the bedroom door behind her. "There's nothing to be scared about, at least not here, in this house."

Then he scooped her into his arms, carried her back to his bed, and set her down in the middle. "We both sleep better when we sleep together," he added, throwing himself down next to her and punching the pillow beneath his cheek. "So close your eyes. Get some sleep."

Easy for him to say, she thought, lying stiff and miserable next to him. She couldn't sleep. Her mind was going a mile a minute. She couldn't forget the mess in her apartment. She couldn't forget the police's indifference. She couldn't forget that Morgan had shown up like a knight on a white stallion.

Suddenly Morgan reached out and scooped her up, bringing her closer against him. "Stop thinking so much," he whispered, his voice raspy in the dark. "Turn your brain off."

"I can't."

"You can. I *order* you to turn your brain off."

She grimaced at the irony. "You can't order me, Morgan. I don't work for you, remember?"

He groaned and dragged her even closer. "Well, I don't want you to work for me. I don't want to be your boss, not when you're my equal." He kissed the back of her head, cupped his hand over her tummy, and immediately relaxed. In less than a minute he began to breathe deeply, evenly.

Winnie turned her head to look at him. His eyes were closed, and his long, dense black lashes rested against his cheek. Even half asleep he was impossibly beautiful.

She felt his breath fan her cheek as he sighed the sigh of a man whose patience was sorely tried. "Close your eyes, Winnie. *Please?*"

"How did you know?" she asked, trying not to laugh.

"Because I know you. Now sleep."

And this time, when she closed her eyes, she did sleep, snuggled deep against Morgan's side.

As tired as he was, Morgan just couldn't sleep. He didn't know how, when he felt completely fatigued, he could still respond to Winnie like this.

She was nestled against him, her cheek on his chest, her hand clenched and buried beneath his ribs. She slept as if he were a mountain, a fortress, her favorite place of refuge and even though he couldn't explain it, it gave him peace.

It was nice to be wanted. He liked being needed. He might even someday grow comfortable with the word love.

For nearly the rest of the night he watched her sleep, and his desire changed as the hours crept by, the hard arousal giving way to something else, a tenderness, a protective instinct.

This, he thought, gently kissing the top of her head, was Winnie, his Winnie. She belonged with him.

Just before five, Morgan finally dragged himself out of bed. He took a cold shower to wake up, then did a cursory shave. The face in the mirror had bloodshot eyes and blue shadows beneath those distinguished red eyes but Morgan felt good. No, he felt great.

But his good feeling didn't last very long. Returning to work was even worse than he expected. The market was down, really down, the big investors were panicking, the traders were running ragged trying to get all the sell orders in. Morgan was just trying to calm the masses, reminding the skittish that markets are cyclical and that even down markets turn around.

But by eleven Morgan couldn't manage his phone

and his nonfunctioning executive assistant's. She was on her third coffee break of the morning—although during one break he could have sworn she was in the ladies' rest room painting her nails.

No, he couldn't manage the phones, the e-mails, the massive stack of market reports and the portfolio managers asking him advice on every new market move.

Morgan dialed his home number. Mr. Foley answered and Morgan asked to speak to Winnie.

Morgan didn't waste any time once she got on the line. "I'm sending the car," he said. "I need you down here, Winnie. I have a one o'clock lunch, a three o'clock meeting, and the office is on the brink of disaster. Can you come immediately?"

CHAPTER TWELVE

"You'll be all right here, while I'm gone?" Morgan asked, slipping his black blazer back on and quickly adjusting his tie.

Winnie couldn't help rolling her eyes. "Of course I will," she said, from her position next to Morgan's desk. She'd spent the last twenty minutes sorting through the papers stacked six inches deep on the corner of his desk.

She'd never seen such an untidy, disorganized collection of phone messages, market reports, printed e-mails and travel itineraries before. Morgan's new assistant was desperately in need of a better filing system. Actually, Morgan was desperately in need of a better assistant.

She lifted a handful of pink phone messages. "So where are you going now?"

"A meeting. Lunch meeting." He lifted his black briefcase from the floor. "I'm not sure how long this will take, but I'll be back by three, in time for the conference call."

He headed out and she continued gathering the pink phone slips before putting them into chronological order. On the bottom went the oldest messages, on the top the newest messages, including everything that had come in today.

The third message from the top caught Winnie's eye.

Charlotte called, confirming lunch. She'll meet you at the Russian Tea Room, one o'clock.

Winnie read the message again. *Charlotte called, confirming lunch.*

It can't be, she told herself. It's not Morgan's Charlotte. It wouldn't be Morgan's Charlotte.

Nonplussed, Winnie stacked the other two messages on top of the one from Charlotte. Her hands shook slightly as she gathered the rest of the messages. She didn't want her imagination to run wild, but she did feel fear. Tremendous fear.

The only woman Morgan had ever loved had been Charlotte. And if Charlotte was back in his life…?

But it's *not* Charlotte.

Don't do this to yourself. Don't make this something it's not.

But her hands were still shaking as she moved on to the next task.

Why would Morgan meet a woman for business at the Tea Room? The Russian Tea Room, now more than seventy years old, was famous for its intimate atmosphere—red leather booths, shiny brass trim, glittering chandeliers. It was a romantic place, a mood place, a place that attracted musicians and artists and actors, *not* businessmen.

Winnie picked up the phone message again. Charlotte. One o'clock. Charlotte. Russian Tea Room. Stomach knotting, she put the message back. It wasn't the old flame Charlotte, it couldn't be. If Morgan were seeing Charlotte at lunch, he'd tell her.

Wouldn't he?

Morgan was late getting back to the office, not returning until quarter past three. Winnie could hardly bring herself to look at him when he finally walked in. He was never late for conference calls, especially not when it involved Shipley's Bank.

She'd agonized about his lunch while he was gone. She'd watched the clock and when two forty-five rolled around and he still wasn't back, she began fretting about his calls. She'd considered phoning him, asking what to do about his calls, but in the end she'd simply rescheduled them both, pushing each call back by an hour.

And that's what she told him when she found her voice. She bit back the reproaches; held in her fear, and acted like the efficient executive assistant he'd once hired her to be. "Morgan, I've rescheduled your three o'clock call to four, and your four o'clock call to five."

But he didn't say thank you. He didn't appear grateful. He simply held out his hand for messages before heading for his office and practically slamming the door closed.

Winnie stared at his closed door. She struggled with her resentment. It wasn't right or fair that he treat her this way. He'd asked *her* to come in today. He'd called *her*, desperate for help.

Give him time, she told herself, fighting for calm. Give him some time and he'll calm down, call you in, and maybe talk about what had happened at lunch.

But he didn't call her in, and he didn't open his door and at a quarter to four, emotions flying high, she opened his office door. "Are you all right?"

He wasn't even working. He sat at his desk but he was facing the window, not his computer. "I'm fine," he said, not bothering to even turn around.

It was like the old days, she thought. The days when he never made eye contact, never acknowledged her, never made her feel like a person.

But things had changed. They were different people now. She knew him, and he wasn't a cold person, or an indifferent person. "Did something happen at lunch?" she asked as gently as possible.

"No."

"But when you left here earlier—"

"Winnie, I really don't want to talk." He swiveled around, his expression closed, eyes shuttered. "No offense, but I'd just like to be alone right now."

Winnie backed out of the office and closed the door. She returned to the desk that had been moved in today for her use and tried to busy herself completing Morgan's expense account, but she couldn't concentrate on the receipts or the form itself. What had happened at lunch? What was he thinking right now?

Suddenly the intercom clicked on. "Winnie, I know you've just rescheduled the calls, but I need you to cancel them. Try to reschedule for tomorrow. Thanks." The intercom clicked off.

Morgan's new assistant looked at her. "Do you want me to do that, Miss Graham?"

Winnie swallowed, knowing how difficult it'd been to get both calls rescheduled once already. "No," she said, fighting frustration. "Let me handle this."

Winnie rolled forward at her desk, pressed the intercom button. "Morgan, it took a great deal of effort to get both calls rescheduled."

"And?"

"And they're going to be even more difficult to reschedule if you cancel them again."

"So your point is?"

She felt herself grow hot. "My point being that maybe you don't want to cancel the conference calls after all. Maybe you want to go ahead and get the calls done so you don't have to hassle with this tomorrow."

"I see." There was a moment of silence over the intercom. Winnie could feel Morgan's new assistant staring at her. The silence wasn't pleasant.

Finally Morgan cleared his throat. "Did I miss something?" he asked. "Did I give you a promotion?"

Her stomach did a flip. "No."

"You haven't been made partner?"

He was a jerk. He was such a jerk. Where was her copy of the book? There had to be a picture of him in the book somewhere. "No, *sir.*"

"Then please don't give me career advice." The intercom clicked off.

Morgan's new assistant was staring at Winnie wide-eyed. "Do you still want to handle it, Miss Graham?"

Winnie grabbed her purse, her summer blazer and her keys from the desk drawer. "No. You take over. You're doing just fine."

Winnie spent an hour walking in Central Park before she finally made her way back to Morgan's apartment.

She didn't want to go to Morgan's place, didn't want to be anywhere near him right now, but she didn't have anywhere else to go. Earlier today Morgan had a moving company pack up everything from Winnie's apartment and put it all into storage until he found her a better place.

She hadn't wanted a new apartment. She hadn't wanted him to send the moving company. But as usual, Morgan won.

Mr. Foley let her in. "Mr. Grady has been phoning every fifteen minutes," the butler said. "He asked that you call when you got in and let him know you're safe."

"I'm safe."

"Well, give him a call. He's anxious to hear from you, and that reminds me, Mr. Grady also mentioned that your mother had phoned. They're staying at a hotel and that number is on a pad of paper in Mr. Grady's study."

In Morgan's office, Winnie turned on the desk lamp and discovered the pad of paper with her mother's name on it, but there were two numbers scribbled down, not one.

Winnie dialed the first number. "Margie Graham, please."

The woman on the other end of the line hesitated. 'I'm sorry. There's no Margie at this number."

"No Grahams registered?"

"This is a private residence. I'm not sure who you're trying to call."

"I'm sorry. I've made a mistake," Winnie said, realizing it must be the second number she was supposed to dial.

"Wait, don't hang up!" The woman drew a short breath. "This is Morgan's number, isn't it?"

Winnie stiffened, muscles snapping like rubber bands in her shoulders and neck. This wasn't right. This didn't feel right and she didn't want to know more. "No," she said. "It's not—"

"But I have Caller ID on my phone. It says Morgan Grady on my phone receiver. You're calling from Morgan's house."

Winnie didn't say anything. Her stomach hurt so bad. Her eyes felt gritty.

"Is this Winnie?"

Winnie slowly sat down in the chair at Morgan's desk. "Who am I speaking to?"

"Charlotte."

Charlotte. *The* Charlotte. Winnie knew.

But Charlotte continued blithely along. "I'm an old friend of Morgan's. We were—"

"College sweethearts. Yes, I know."

"Right." Charlotte laughed a little, but it sounded strained. "Listen, Morgan left his briefcase at the restaurant after lunch. Let him know I'll just drop it off later today."

"Here, or at the office?" Winnie asked, hating the tightness in her chest, hating the dull panic. Morgan had only loved Charlotte and Charlotte was definitely back in his life. Peripheral or not, Charlotte was a threat.

"Does it matter?" And Charlotte laughed again, another small brittle laugh that made Winnie feel very cold, and very afraid.

Winnie paced her bedroom, heart racing so fast she couldn't get any air.

God, she was a fool. A dolt. A royal idiot. She couldn't do anything right, couldn't make anything work.

She hated this awful claustrophobic feeling, hated the

roar in her head, the crazy adrenaline in her veins. Until the wedding she hadn't had a panic attack in years, and now she'd had two in less than ten days.

All because of Morgan.

Morgan, Wall Street's Most Eligible Bachelor.

All because she'd goofed with him, hadn't been able to get it right, couldn't make the relationship work.

He'd wanted cool. She gave him hot. He wanted reason. She lived in illogic. He used the minimum words and she talked in a steady stream, all words, all the time, words nonstop.

Back in seventh grade Winnie had panic attacks regularly, at least one a week, sometimes one a day. She dreaded everything about school, feared speaking in class, was terrified of P.E.

Softball was the worst. She hated, hated, hated the game. The big hard ball always flew at her face... Her glasses would slip low on her nose and because she couldn't see the ball coming at her, she would swing before the ball smashed into her. Sometimes she would duck before the ball crossed the plate, duck and drop the bat.

The kids all laughed. Even the P.E. teacher laughed.

Ninny Winnie. Winnie Graham who couldn't do anything right.

A knock sounded on her bedroom door and Winnie stopped pacing long enough to answer the door.

"I'm leaving for the evening," Mr. Foley said. He had Monday nights off and usually went to visit his sister on Long Island. He turned a little, noted her suitcase sitting by the door. "You're leaving?"

Her eyes burned. She felt terrible on the inside, just

like she used to feel as a girl. "I'm going to go see my mom."

"That sounds like a nice break." Winnie nodded jerkily. Mr. Foley's brown eyes narrowed a little, his expression immensely kind. "Mr. Grady is a very private person, very protective of his personal life. He's never brought anyone here before. You're the first."

"He didn't have much of a choice. My door was pretty well smashed in. He couldn't very well leave me there."

"But he could have taken you to his penthouse just off Wall Street. That's where he usually entertains. But this is his home and he brought you here."

Mr. Foley paused, gave her time to digest this before adding, "I don't know what he's said, or not said, but I've worked for Mr. Grady for a number of years. One thing you need to know is that when it comes to Mr. Grady, actions speak louder than words."

His gaze leveled with hers. "Would you like me to call a cab for you, or are you going to wait for Mr. Grady?"

Heart in her throat, chest filled with longing, she looked away, across her bedroom. He'd put her in the guest room but welcomed her into his bed. Did he love her, or just need her? She didn't know. But she had to find out. "I'll wait."

Morgan brought Chinese food home with him from a local take-out. They sat in his family room, facing each other at opposite ends of the couch. She didn't know how he knew, but Morgan had ordered everything she liked best. Mongolian beef. Kung Pao chicken.

Sweet and sour pork. But she couldn't eat any of it, couldn't even get her chopsticks to work.

"You left early," Morgan said, no problem with his appetite, taking seconds of nearly everything.

There'd be no Valentines with this man. No chocolate-covered cherries. He'd proposed to her because she was the best option. She filled the job. She was the most qualified candidate. No romance there.

"Do you ever think about Charlotte?" she asked, setting her chopsticks down. "Do you ever wonder what it'd be like if you and she were still together?"

"We were talking about work."

She pushed her plate aside. "I'd rather talk about us."

"Charlotte's not 'us.' Charlotte is Charlotte."

Winnie knew she was heading into troubled waters but she couldn't avoid this, couldn't ignore this. She had to understand, had to know why he could love Charlotte but not her. "Just tell me one thing—when you proposed to her, what were you feeling?"

Morgan clamped his jaw tight, battling his mounting frustration. How could he have ever thought Winnie coolly unemotional? How could he have thought her reasonable? "You really don't want to do this—"

"But I do."

"Winnie, I can't play games. I can't make up stories. I don't want to hurt you, either. Why compare Charlotte to you? It's like comparing apples to oranges."

Her chin lifted, hazel eyes bright with tears. "Am I the apple or the orange?"

He couldn't even crack a smile. His blood pressure was shooting up. "You want the truth? Fine. Here's the truth. I did love Charlotte, I loved her a lot. She was my first real girlfriend, my first true love affair. Everything with her had been stormy, passionate, and intense. I thought we'd spend the rest of our lives together.''

Morgan drew a deep breath, gritted his teeth. He couldn't believe he was even talking about this out loud, couldn't believe he'd touch this deeply private pain. Seeing Charlotte today had been bad enough. He'd realized all over again how little he'd known her, how little he'd understood how her mind worked.

She'd never loved him, just the idea of him. She'd never wanted him, but the Grady name and the Grady connections. She'd been sickened that he had been adopted at fifteen.

What kind of person gets adopted as a teenager? she'd asked. *You adopt babies, toddlers, you raise them from birth. You can't adopt a teenager.*

Who are your parents anyway? What kind of people give away a fifteen-year-old?

''I thought it was love, Winnie,'' he said coldly, all emotion bottled inside him, smashed hard into a place he couldn't touch. ''But it wasn't love. It was sex.''

''Just like us.'' A tear slid down Winnie's cheek. She batted it away.

She was wrong, Morgan thought, but he didn't have the energy to argue. He'd learned years ago that people couldn't make other people happy. Happiness had to come from within. Happiness had to be a personal choice.

''We have great sex, but we also have a real friendship,'' he said at last, so glad he'd seen Charlotte today and realized that perhaps the thing he'd loved most about Charlotte was her attitude.

He'd adored her rich-girl diction, her perfect blond bob, her narrow straight nose lifted disdainfully at the world. He'd loved that she, beautiful, regal, rich Charlotte, had wanted *him*. In retrospect, he'd been just as selfish as she. Thank God, Charlotte had broken the wedding off. She'd done them both the greatest favor.

Morgan drew a slow breath. "Even if the sex was bad, the friendship is worth saving. We have a lot here. We have a lot going for us. It'd be foolish to make decisions based on a very narrow definition of love."

Winnie didn't know what to think. She was a romantic. He a pragmatist. She craved bonbons, flowers, violins and he lived in a stark reality minus all those things. She loved the way he touched her, but hated his vision of love. How could this work? How could they ever compromise?

Yet how could she compromise if she didn't trust him? Winnie drew a deep breath. "Who did you have lunch with?"

He looked up at her, his eyes narrowing. There was a strange beat, a moment of silence that felt like a great divide. "Charlotte." There was another silence, this one shorter. "But you already knew that, didn't you?"

When Winnie didn't answer, Morgan sighed. "This is why it won't work, having you as my assistant. A lot of things happened today that shouldn't have happened. I get a lot of calls. I see a lot of people. I need to make quick decisions and I shouldn't have to explain myself, or defend myself—"

"Then don't!" Winnie finally understood why she

couldn't continue at Grady Investments. Morgan had his life. He'd always had his own life. She'd just never known about it before.

"It's not an issue of trust, but of energy and time. You're a great executive assistant. The best I've ever had—"

"I got it. Thanks." He didn't need to repeat himself, she thought bitterly. She wasn't stupid. "I already said I understood."

Winnie's nerves stretched, pulled far too taut. She had to get out of here. Had to get some time to herself, needed to get her head back in the right place. "You said you'd given me a three month severance package, well, I think I'll take advantage of it and not work for a while. I might leave the city for a while, go spend some time with my family."

He didn't say anything for a moment. She'd expected him to nod, give his approval. Instead he looked at her, his expression surprisingly bleak. "How long do you intend to be gone?"

She wanted him to say, "No, don't go." She wanted him to say, "Stay here with me." She wanted him to say something emotional, something powerful, something indicating his true feelings. His expression was one thing, but she really needed words.

But he didn't say anything else, didn't try to talk her into staying.

Winnie stared at his eyes, his mouth, the faint lines etched on either side of those remarkable lips. She felt the worst kind of sorrow. Wanted so badly to be with him but didn't know how to make it work anymore. "I don't know. Just depends on what I feel like doing. I'm already packed. I'm heading out tonight.''

Morgan's intensely blue eyes met hers. ''Well then, I better give you this now.''

He reached into his pocket and withdrew a small gold key chain with three shiny keys. ''Your new place. I bought it for you. I picked up the keys from the Realtor today, after my thirty-minute lunch with Charlotte. I was late getting back to the office because the paperwork took longer than we expected.''

CHAPTER THIRTEEN

WINNIE emptied her bag of groceries in the kitchen of her new apartment, which was part of an elegant brownstone building on a lovely tree-lined street.

She'd been back in the city nearly a week now, after having been gone for a month. She'd spent her first week away with her parents, then a week with her sister Alexis, and then the last two weeks traveling on her own.

She'd told herself she was visiting all the historic places on the southeastern seaboard she'd always wanted to see, but the truth was she was avoiding New York. Avoiding returning. Avoiding, most of all, Morgan.

But she couldn't stay away forever. She lived in New York. Her life was in New York—even if her life wasn't with Morgan Grady.

Winnie put the milk in her refrigerator and the bread on the counter. She'd bought some fresh flowers, so she cut the bottoms of the stems off and then put them in water. Hard to believe, she thought, arranging the dahlias, that they were already in the last week of August. A late Saturday afternoon and summer was nearly over.

Time to start looking for work. She needed a job. Something to do.

Something other than pining for Morgan.

Because she did pine for him. She felt like a woman

from a Victorian novel, felt as if she'd had a taste of heaven and she'd turned around and run the other way.

Someday she'd get it figured out. Someday she'd meet someone like her, someone kind of goofy and absurd, someone sentimental and deeply emotional and they'd make this perfect life together.

But until then, a job would help fill all her empty hours.

Winnie placed the flowers on her dining table and reached for the newspaper. Sitting cross-legged on her couch, she opened up the paper but hadn't even reached the Classifieds when her doorbell rang.

Winnie peered through the peephole.

Morgan. He was dressed in black tie—black tuxedo, elegant white shirt and white silk bow tie.

She unlocked the door and swung it open. "Hi."

Mercy, he was beautiful. She leaned against the door, unable to tear her gaze away. The tuxedo made him look taller, shoulders even broader, and she could smell his cologne. It was rich with vanilla and spice and perfect with a tuxedo.

"I found your glasses," he said. "I thought you might need them back."

She couldn't bring herself to take them, was terribly afraid of what she'd feel if she touched him. "I pretty much only wear my contacts now."

"I liked you in your glasses."

"They're ugly."

"They make you look brainy." His lips twisted, creases at his eyes. "Not that you need glasses to look brainy. You're one of the smartest women I've ever met."

Her heart ached. "Thank you." Winnie shifted her weight from one foot to the other. Her pulse raced. "Where are you going?"

"The Faith Foundation's Charity Ball."

"I thought you hated those things."

His smile turned self-deprecating. "I do, but I'm co-sponsor. This is the event each year I have to attend."

"Well, you look incredible," she said, quickly taking the glasses from him, being extra careful so their fingers didn't brush. "If that's any consolation."

His gaze met hers and held. "It's not a consolation if I have to go alone."

Oh, that hurt. She hurt. She didn't want him to go alone. She wanted to go with him. But how would this work? Where would things go? Winnie couldn't bear to think of a future always wondering, worrying, doubting. She needed to be sure of Morgan. Needed to be certain of how he felt. "Where's the party?"

"The Met museum." He reached out, and very gently touched her cheek. "Come with me tonight."

She didn't say yes, she didn't say no. She just stared at him.

"Just a moment," he said, turning around and heading back to the elevator. He returned a moment later and thrust a box at her. The box was slim and taupe-colored and tied with a narrow gold ribbon. "I didn't want you to say you wouldn't come because you had nothing to wear."

"Morgan—" she whispered his name.

"If you're going to say no, I wanted to make sure you were saying no because of me."

She looked away, and her fingers tightened around

the slender box. It weighed virtually nothing. That meant whatever was inside weighed even less than nothing. She'd recognized the name printed on the box. It was a very expensive, very exclusive boutique that carried only designer labels from France and Italy.

"I can't," she said softly. "It wouldn't be right." Yet even as she said the words, she could imagine the limo downstairs, probably champagne on ice. They'd have a drink in the car on the way there and then they'd pull up at the museum and…

They'd immediately be surrounded by photographers. The press would be there. The scrutiny would start. The world would pick at her, criticize her, and she couldn't handle it, couldn't endure it if she was just the latest in Morgan Grady's string of lovers.

She wanted more.

She wanted forever.

Winnie tried to hand the dress back. "I'm not black-tie material."

His mouth compressed, deep grooves forming next to his mouth. "You don't even let yourself see the possibilities."

Her eyes burned and she blinked. "It's not that I don't see the possibilities, but I also see the reality. We want different things, Morgan."

His blue gaze searched her eyes. "Not as different as you might think."

She couldn't speak, didn't trust herself to say the right words. She was never concise, or intelligent when she felt so much. Instead she simply shook her head and pressed the box firmly into Morgan's hands.

But he'd have none of it. Swearing, he tossed the box

past her, into the living room where it skidded across the floor. And then he just walked away.

Winnie returned to the couch, curled up in one corner and felt absolutely sick.

She felt sick because she knew she was wrong sending him off without her. She felt sick because she was making choices out of fear. She felt sick because she knew she was just a big fat coward.

Just like she'd been a coward most of her life.

She hadn't been confident as a child. Her panic attacks were a testament to that. But instead of ever conquering her fear, she'd slowly let it get the best of her.

She gave up on sports early. She never tried out for cheerleading. She wouldn't audition for a spelling bee or the school plays.

In college she didn't date. How could she? Except for class, she never left her dorm room.

Her very first job interview was botched, and so instead of trying again, she gave up the career she'd really wanted.

And now she was giving up on the one man she wanted.

Tonight Morgan appeared on her doorstep. He'd bought her a dress. He asked her to join him. Yet what had she done? She'd handed the dress back and said no.

She'd said no because she was afraid. She'd said no because she was terrified she'd love him so much and he'd love her not enough and in the end she'd just look like a fool.

How insecure was that? She cared more about her

fragile heart than trying to make a relationship with Morgan work.

Far better to be the injured party. Far better to play victim. Far better to be a dreamy romantic than a confident woman willing to take a risk.

Grow up, Winnie. Stop wanting everything to be perfect. You already have the fairy tale!

Winnie stooped and picked up the garment box from the ground. Cradling the box on her lap, she opened the lid, pushed back the thin gold tissue paper and drew out a silk camisole the color of ripe bananas, and a lovely long narrow skirt of matching yellow silk with a pale gold overlay stitched with gold and purple jewels.

She blinked, tears starting to her eyes. The dress looked like a banana daiquiri on a sun-kissed beach.

He'd given her a taste of paradise.

For a moment she couldn't breathe, concentrating hard on not blinking and keeping the tears from falling. She didn't want to get any tears on the silk fabric. Didn't want anything to ruin the most beautiful, magical dress she'd ever seen.

She had to go. She had to be there tonight. She had to show him she was ready for a real relationship with him. One built on friendship, honesty, admiration, and trust. Incredibly dull virtues on paper but extraordinary in real life.

Winnie carried the silk camisole with the beaded straps and skirt to her bedroom, held the two-piece dress against her as she looked at her reflection in her bedroom mirror. Beautiful. How had he known that this was absolutely the most perfect dress for her?

Because he knew her.

Because his actions spoke louder than words.

Winnie pressed her forehead to the painted trim around the door and squeezed back the tears threatening to spill.

Actions, not words.

He'd proposed. He'd taken her to St. Jermaine's. He'd held her every night. He'd hired security for her. Bought her a house.

He was saying as best as he could that she was his, that he wanted her, that he needed her.

And for heaven's sake, wasn't that enough?

Need and want…how was it so different from love?

Morgan said the brief speech he'd prepared, a few positive words about the foster care system and a short but sincere thank-you to those who'd come that night and supported the program.

He was leaving the podium, shaking outstretched hands, and yet his gaze was never far from the door. He hated these things, hated the show and the dress-up and the facade he wore to keep everyone happy. People, he knew, preferred success.

People preferred handsome, rich, polished. Not that he felt that way underneath. Hell, underneath he was one lonely and very alone billionaire.

Almost done, he told himself, seeing a bit of space near the door. Shake a few more hands, pretend to get a drink, and then make a mad dash for the limo.

He was still moving forward, and nearly at the museum's glass doors when he cast one last glance around the perimeter of the lobby, his gaze taking in the tux-

edos and black sheathlike dresses, before spotting ca-
nary yellow.

Yellow. His yellow.

Her back was to him. She was looking the other way.
She'd pinned her long hair partway back, curled the
rest, and a few soft tendrils framed her face. The purple
beaded straps on her camisole glittered in the party
lights and yet he knew the yellow because it was the
right yellow, it was the yellow of sunshine, warmth and
happiness.

Morgan stood transfixed, drinking her in. He felt the
fullness of the summer, the sweetness of the island, and
far from urban problems. He felt again the days when
he'd just been adopted by the Gradys and he felt such
gratitude, and hope.

Hope.

As he watched, Winnie's smooth brow creased. Her
eyes narrowed as she searched the room, lower lip
caught between her teeth.

She was looking for him.

His chest tightened and Morgan knew without a
doubt that he'd never tire of the summer. Or the sun.

And he'd never tire of Winnie.

Quickly, he pushed through the crowd lining up at
the bar, lifted a hand in acknowledgment as someone
called his name, sidestepped a reporter interviewing a
charity patron. Winnie was moving in the opposite direction, heading to the exit, out of the ballroom.

He reached her at the great stone archway, stretched
out a hand, and touched the back of her bare warm
shoulder. ''Winnie.''

Heat shot through her, heat and pleasure. Winnie

turned, stomach knotting, lower lip raw from being anxiously gnawed. "I couldn't find you."

"How long have you been here?"

"A half hour. I couldn't find you, and then someone said they'd seen you head to the exit, that you were doing the usual Grady move of sneaking out."

"I was."

"I almost missed you—" She broke off, hazel eyes darkening with silent emotion. "I almost missed everything."

"You've missed nothing."

There was so much tenderness in his voice. Her lip quivered as she fought the intensity of her feelings. "I'm sorry I didn't come with you. I'm sorry I made this whole thing so difficult—"

"You're here now. That's enough. And you look…" He shook his head, pride in his eyes. "Beautiful."

She touched her hips a little self-consciously. The delicate skirt hugged her curves and fell in a shimmer of yellow and gold to her feet. "It's the dress." But she liked the compliment, appreciated the compliment. He made her feel so incredible. "Do you still want company tonight?"

His blue eyes darkened, the navy almost ink. "More than ever."

Winnie woke up to the sound of the sea. Her eyes fluttered open and for a moment she looked at the ceiling not knowing where she was.

Then the waves crashed again, breaking on the sand, and Morgan's arm reached out, extended across her belly before moving up to cup her breast. "I missed this." His voice sounded low and husky. "I missed you."

Winnie rolled over on her side. They'd gone to bed last night with the doors open and now sunlight and fresh air filled the room. They'd left New York Sunday morning to spend a few stolen days on St. Jermaine's.

Winnie loved the feel of his hand on her breast, but more than anything, loved the warmth in his eyes. He did care for her. He cared for her so very much. "You missed me?" she repeated smiling faintly.

"Quite a bit."

"I guess in Morgan speak, that means the same thing as I love you."

His lips twitched. A day-old beard darkened his jaw. His teeth flashed in an easy white smile. "Is there something wrong with Morgan speak?"

Her smile grew; the smile starting on the inside, in her chest, where her heart felt warm, where happiness was made. "There's absolutely nothing wrong with Morgan speak. You say as little as you want. I'll happily fill in the gaps."

He chuckled softly, appreciatively. "You're very funny."

"Absolutely hilarious. In my next career I'll be a standup comedian."

"You remembered."

"I remember everything."

His lips curved, his eyes smiled, a sheen on the gorgeous sapphire blues. "So let's see, regarding your grasp on Morgan speak, if I say, I love pancakes..."

"It really means no one makes better pancakes than Winnie."

"If I say, I like spending time with you?"

"It translates to 'I can't imagine ever living without you.'"

His husky laugh filled the room and leaning forward, he kissed her very slowly. "I love you, Winnie."

Did he just say that? Did he say the words?

Her eyes burned and the ache in her chest was so intense she couldn't distinguish between joy and pain.

"So, Winnie, translate that one for me."

She couldn't.

She, who had a million words at her disposal, couldn't think of one. He'd just blown her away.

"Well, smarty pants," he said softly, reaching out to lift a tendril of hair from her cheek. "I'll tell you what it means. It means, I love you, I love you, I love you. Got it?"

Her lips quivered and a tear spilled over. She didn't want to cry. She really didn't want to cry. This was the best moment of her whole life and tears were for the birds. "I think so. But you might want to say it one more time just to be sure I really, completely understand."

He shifted his weight, moved on top of her. His head dipped, his lips brushed her ear. "I love you, Winnie Graham, and only you, Winnie Graham. Will you please spend the rest of your life with me?"

"Yes."

He gave her a look of mock surprise. "What? No argument. No questions about my sincerity, or the kind of role you're going to play?"

"No." She blinked and more tears spilled. "No argument. No questions." The tears trickled down her cheek, past her mouth. She could taste the wet salty dampness on the corner of her lips. "And absolutely no doubts. You love me. That's enough for me. It's all I need to know."

Later in the afternoon, after amazing sex, great food served by an extremely chipper Mr. Foley, and more amazing sex, they'd straggled down to the beach to get some sun.

Winnie lay on her beach towel, smiling up at the sky. Paradise. She'd found paradise but she'd discovered something about paradise. It wasn't an island, or a concept. It wasn't a place. It wasn't even being with Morgan.

It was just being okay with yourself. Not being so afraid of yourself. Of accepting the good with the bad and learning to accept others the same way.

"There's an opening at the office," Morgan said from his beach lounge chair, tossing aside his newspaper.

The turquoise water lapped at the white sand, and without a breeze there were hardly any waves in the small crescent bay. Winnie shaded her eyes as she looked at him. "You want me to go back to work?"

"I thought you wanted to go back to work."

She was a bit puzzled by the direction of the conversation. "I do miss the office."

"So call and schedule an interview."

"You're going to make me go through an interview?"

"You think you should get special advantages just because you're the boss's girlfriend?"

She threw her bikini top at him. "I'm not your girl-friend. I'm your mistress. Remember?"

Morgan's dark blue eyes narrowed as they swept over her light gold skin. She was naked except for her yellow bikini bottoms. "Mmm, I'm remembering."

She knew where his mind was headed but she wanted more information from him first. "Tell me about the job. How long has the position been open? Who would I work with?"

Morgan handed her a section of the paper. "It's in here. We've been running the advertisement in Classifieds all week. Résumés are pouring in."

Winnie's gaze swept the narrow columns. "Nothing here for administrative assistants."

"You're on the wrong page. Check under business, marketing."

That's weird, she thought, but she flipped the paper to the page he'd said. Her eyes scanned the ads then rested on one. "It's a market research position."

"The first we've had in nearly five years." His eyes met hers. "The first since you walked out of the inter-view at Grady Investments nearly five years ago."

For a long moment Winnie didn't speak, her gaze fixed on the tranquil turquoise water and the darker patches of purple indicating submerged beds of coral.

She drew a slow breath. "How did you know I interviewed for an analyst position?"

"It was in your employment file. I discovered it when Mr. Osborne called to check on your references."

He'd known this about her for months and yet he'd never said a thing until now. "Why didn't you tell me you knew?"

"I was waiting for you to tell me yourself." He reached out, clasped her hand and tugged her off her towel and onto his chair.

She felt nervous now, and she scrambled to get her bikini top on. "Told you what? That I panicked in your conference room and made a total fool of myself?"

"You'd make a great market analyst, Winnie. I want you to interview."

Her eyes were burning again. She adjusted her suit, blinked, and focused on the house with its pots of red and pink hibiscus, the trailing purple bougainvillea, and the tall arching coconut trees. "I thought you didn't want me to work at your office. I thought you didn't want to work with me."

"For such a smart girl, you've got it all wrong. I didn't want you to work *for* me. I want you to work *with* me. I know it's only a little preposition, but it's an important one."

EPILOGUE

One month later

THE bathroom was steamy and fragrant with Morgan's aftershave. Winnie rose on tiptoe and leaned across the wide marble counter to grab the toothpaste. But even on her toes it was still out of reach.

Morgan bumped her with his hip. "Hey, stay on your own side."

"I am on my side. My toothpaste just happens to be on your side."

"And how did that happen?"

"Because you borrowed it," she flashed, finally able to scoot past his very solid torso and snatch the tube back. Yet in reaching past him she got a glimpse of his taut abdomen. He hadn't buttoned his dress shirt yet and she was unable to resist the lovely flat bands of muscle cut across his stomach.

Winnie pushed his shirt open wider and pressed a kiss to his warm, toned belly. He inhaled quickly and she smiled to herself and kissed him an inch lower before tracing his hard muscle with the tip of her tongue.

He shuddered at the caress. "Winnie, we don't have time."

She loved the feel of his body, loved the way she turned him on. "Sure, we do," she whispered wickedly before kissing him again, lower this time, her mouth finding him through his Italian-cut trousers.

He caught her head in his heads, his fingers sliding through her loose hair. "You make me crazy."

"Good."

Muttering an oath, Morgan reached down, picked her up from the floor and placed her on the edge of the counter.

She felt a thrill of excitement. "We're going to be late," she mocked, heart racing, eyes shining, loving the adventure of life with Morgan Grady.

"Your fault," he said, parting her knees, pushing up her slim skirt and stepping between her thighs. He slid her body forward and she felt his arousal, his body so hard it made her instantly weak.

Winnie drew Morgan's face down to hers. "Kiss me."

"I'll never stop."

"You'll have to. It's my first day of work."

His lips touched hers and shocks of energy jumped through her. Just one kiss and she felt hot and electric. One touch and she knew she'd always feel wildly passionate about this man.

"You should have thought about that before you started playing dangerous games," he retorted, sliding his hands up to cup her breasts.

She sighed with pleasure, sinking closer to him. "I'm going to get fired before I even get the office tour."

He kissed the side of her neck, just below her ear. "You don't need the office tour. You already know your way around the Tower building's seventy-eighth floor."

Winnie closed her eyes, savoring the feel of his mouth against her skin and she lifted her chin higher to give him better access to her skin. "But how would it look if Grady Investments' newest research analyst showed up late on her first day? Everyone would think I'm taking advantage of my special relationship with the boss.''

His lips had found the very secret, very sensitive spot where all her nerve endings seemed to come together. All it took was just one touch there and she forgot everything—duty, reason, responsibility.

Morgan lifted his head, gazed down into her warm, flushed face even as he slid his hands beneath her blouse and unclasped her bra. ''Speaking of your special relationship with the boss, I think it's time we changed the status quo.''

''You do?'' she answered breathlessly, cool air hitting her aching breasts.

''Yes. I can't have all the men hitting on the company's brainy new analyst.''

''So, boss, what do you propose?''

''Marry me.''

She sat up, stared deep into his blue eyes. They were the most beautiful color she'd ever seen. ''Marry you?''

''Unless you're afraid of making me a long-term commitment.'' His smile slipped and he leaned forward to clasp her face in his hands, his expression serious. ''Are you?''

''No. Oh, Morgan, no. You're the love of my life, the sun in my sky. You're my very own Prince Charming.''

''So we try the wedding thing again?''

She wiggled closer and wrapped her arms around his neck. ''Can we just skip the big white wedding, have a quiet little ceremony on the island, then jump to the happy-ever-after part?''

His incredible blue eyes, still the sexiest blue eyes in all of Manhattan, creased with love and silent laughter.

"You drive a hard bargain for a princess, but you've got yourself a deal," he said, before kissing her senseless.

Happily for all, Winnie still managed to make it to her first day of work as a research analyst on time.

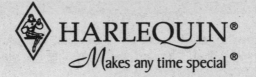

HARLEQUIN®
Makes any time special®

HARLEQUIN®
AMERICAN *Romance*

Upbeat, All-American Romances

HARLEQUIN®
Duets™

Romantic Comedy

HARLEQUIN®
Harlequin® *Historical*

Historical, Romantic Adventure

HARLEQUIN®
INTRIGUE

Romantic Suspense

Harlequin Romance®

Capturing the World You Dream Of

HARLEQUIN®
Presents

Seduction and passion guaranteed

HARLEQUIN® *Super*ROMANCE®

Emotional, Exciting, Unexpected

HARLEQUIN®
Temptation

Sassy, Sexy, Seductive!

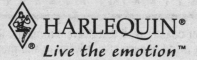

❤ *Silhouette*®

SILHOUETTE *Romance*.

From first love to forever, these love stories
are fairy tale romances for today's woman.

❤ *Silhouette*® *Desire*.

Modern, passionate reads that are powerful and provocative.

❤ *Silhouette*® SPECIAL EDITION™

Emotional, compelling stories that capture the intensity
of living, loving and creating a family in today's world.

❤ *Silhouette*® INTIMATE MOMENTS™

A roller-coaster read that delivers romantic thrills
in a world of suspense, adventure and more.

SDIR204

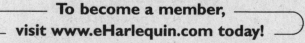

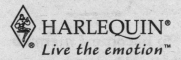